Finding Forever in Sweet Berry Cove

Sweet Berry Cove, Volume 2

Ness Woodberry

Published by Lynda French, 2025.

FINDING FOREVER IN SWEET BERRY COVE

First edition. October 10, 2025.

Written by Ness Woodberry.

Also by Ness Woodberry

Sweet Berry Cove
Finding Forever in Sweet Berry Cove

Standalone
Finding Love in Sweet Berry Cove

Table of Contents

To those who chase their heart's desire.

Book Description

This book continues the story of Milly and Daniel from "Finding Love in Sweet Berry Cove".

Milly found love in Sweet Berry Cove but did love find her? she feels a little romancing would go a long way to make her believe she's more than just a convenient, practical solution.

Daniel isn't a mind-reader, and Milly's schemes all backfire on her, but when two people find their forever love is it strong enough to defeat their fears and flaws?

Familiar characters, from the inquisitive to the charitable, return in this wholesome story where family togetherness fosters the Christmas spirit.

The small town of Sweet Berry Cove celebrates the festive season with parties, dances, and - after a few hiccups - plenty of goodwill.

The holiday magic of this heartwarming tale will linger along with the joy of its happily ever after.

Milly Has Regrets

If only fairy tales came true... if only there really was such a thing as happily ever after, sighs Milly. She's taking the dog for a walk and this overcast, gray morning suits her gloomy mood. *I'm morose,* she tells herself savoring a word she's read, but never heard in real-life conversation.

Usually Milly is a cheerful young woman with a bright outlook. Now, she's not sure what to do. She feels fretful so she's chosen to hide herself from everyone in the family. At least until her sadness goes away.

A fruit farm by the ocean in December is a cold, closed place. An orchard of leafless trees, a field of burlap bundles, and no color in a place that recently was bathed in warm harvest hues. *It's as dull and dreary as me,* Milly tells herself, wallowing in self-pity.

Bernie, the Young's Saint Bernard puppy, senses that his mistress is unhappy. He whines a little and licks her hand in comfort, but he's still a puppy and easily distracted by a movement in the bushes up ahead.

It's only a Monarch butterfly, but Bernie is entranced watching it flit and dart, flying here and there, just out of his reach. He looks so clumsy trying to catch it and his jumping only ends up landing him in the bush.

If Milly had kept her eye on the dog she'd be smiling at his antics. Instead, her attention is fully devoted to feeling regretful and castigating herself.

Milly wishes she'd never manipulated Daniel into declaring himself because now it feels like their love story has become a business arrangement. With another mournful sigh she realizes she's only got herself to blame.

Why was I so impatient? I knew how he felt from what I overheard but I just couldn't let myself wait for him to speak to me in his own time. No, I had to play games... and trick him.

It seemed like such a cute bit of play-acting at the time, having a fake conversation with Bernie as a roundabout way to let Daniel know she returned his feelings. It prompted him to give her her very first kiss, but it backfired.

Let's see, today is December 16 so that kiss happened more than a month ago! We've kissed since, she pauses a moment for a pleasant recollection of them kissing a lot at Thanksgiving.

But that was three weeks ago and Milly believes Daniel is already taking it for granted that they'll marry and live in the Young farmhouse.

Marry the employee and get the labor for free. She makes a *hmmph* sound, knowing she's being ridiculously dramatic. The situation isn't that bad but... he's never bothered to actually propose.

Am I being silly? she wonders. *I wish I could talk to Nora about this stuff, she and Amos are very happy together and I value her opinion but... I can't bear to let on how insecure I am deep down.*

Although Milly is inexperienced in the ways of love she understands Daniel well-enough to know that he isn't the *grand gesture* type. Still, she hoped for – expected, actually – much more than this pragmatic approach. She can't help feeling disappointed. It's all very practical and sensible and she hates it.

Where is the romance? where are the starry eyes, hearts and flowers, and passionate kisses? Is my courtship over already? she worries.

There's no question that Daniel has my heart but... she shakes her head at herself. *There's no but about it, no need to be sad or disappointed. Daniel*

2

is the one for me and this is just the way things are, it's his way. He's really never been much of a talker and I know that.

Straightening her shoulders as if shoring up her resolve Milly whistles for Bernie to come back then she turns to head home.

For some reason Helena Larch, Daniel's ex-fiancée, comes to mind with Milly wondering how that engagement came about. She can't imagine Daniel getting down on one knee but then she's can't picture him as a teenager, either. He seems such a complete, confident man.

And he's not going to want a shy, insipid girl constantly in need of reassurance. I have to give up on these immature romantic fantasies of mine and be strong and practical, just like he is.

The air has turned chilly now that the wind's picked up blowing away the early mist. It pushes against her back, hurrying her to return to the warmth of the farmhouse to prepare the family's breakfast.

A Pastoral Visit

Walking up the hill to the manse Reverend Stephen Smithson is rueful. When he heard Helena Larch was back in Sweet Berry Cove he'd hoped she and Daniel Young might rekindle their affair. Stephen didn't live here when those two were an item, but by all accounts they'd had a passionate, on-again/off-again relationship.

He figured if they got back together then he'd have a chance with Milly Clarke. *I should be ashamed of myself for even thinking that way,* he silently admonishes, *except I do believe that all's fair in love and war, and Milly is simply lovely. And she doesn't even realize just how beautiful she is, inside and out.*

But it turns out there's no chance of a reunion between the erstwhile lovers. Helena is obviously still very much in love with her estranged husband, Christopher, as the Reverend discovered on his pastoral visit with her and her mother, Martha Hannaford. Helena has recently moved back home and The Cove's gossip mill is churning.

Stephen can see that the women are struggling with the burden of their thoughts and worries. He knows they won't relax sitting upright in the living-room so he insists the three of them move to the kitchen to drink their mid-morning coffee. After the first sip he remembers that Martha Hannaford always brewed a weak cup, no doubt a habit after years of penny-pinching.

Taking a wafer cookie from the plate he remarks: "I haven't had one of these in years. I never really cared for the chocolate flavor but I always enjoyed the vanilla and this, the strawberry one, is my favorite." He munches the slightly stale cookie while giving the mother and daughter a friendly and encouraging look.

Stephen is hopeful the young couple will work through this difficult time, contrary to the dire prediction of *marry in haste, repent at leisure* spoken by the local busybodies.

Helena Hannaford wasn't popular with the ladies of Sweet Berry Cove who called her *grasping and greedy*, and *a selfish, dissatisfied girl*. Meeting Helena was enlightening. Stephen was pleased to discover the existence of a kinder, gentler side to the young woman.

Helena and her Chris, as she calls him, have to deal with an unforeseen circumstance that is shocking. Stephen wonders what the gossips of this place will say once the whole story comes out.

I can only imagine! he thinks, speculating. *But Helena's faith in her husband has been shaken, not broken, and I think she'll pass this test with grace.* The tearful young woman, who he met for the first time today, is nothing like what he expected based on the rumors he'd heard.

Although it's true that she does seem very money-oriented, he concludes thinking that the couple's financial situation is a justifiable concern. In his role as *The Reverend Smithson* Stephen counseled according to the Christian precepts of the Calvary Church with Helena and Martha nodding along at his words, but what resonated with the girl was his suggestion that she *sit down for a heart-to-heart chat with Samuel Young.*

"Samuel told me how well the two of you always got along. If you still value his advice then I think you'll find comfort discussing this with him, and I'm sure he'll help you see your way forward."

In fact Samuel had told Stephen that the Helena Hannaford he knew was a sweet and very likeable girl, quite different from the impression she gave in public.

"Oh! Oh Mr. Young was like a second father to me!" exclaims Helena. "Even after, you know, Daniel and I split up, Mr. Young was always so kind. He always had time to listen..." she trails off and it's obvious her thoughts have gone back in recollection.

Her small smile grows into an enthusiastic grin when she grabs Stephen's hands saying: "That's a wonderful idea, thank you so much, Reverend Smithson!"

Her mother agrees: "Yes, thank you Reverend. Samuel Young has always been a good friend to our family and I'm sure he'll give Helena good, helpful advice."

Stephen sighs as he replays their conversation over in his mind while he heads home. There's no chance that Helena will try to lure Daniel away from Milly. *And even if she did there's no guarantee that Milly would look twice at me!* he reminds himself. At the top of the hill he continues past his home and goes into the Church where he'll sit in quiet meditation until he feels peaceful again.

The Cove's gossip grapevine is soon discussing Reverend Smithson's visit to the Hannaford residence. Speculation grows wild since there are no facts to keep it in check.

Later on, when Helena Larch is seen going to the Young's farmhouse, old rumors are dusted off to be revisited with interest.

Nesting

After helping Hannah clear away the lunch things Nora comes out of the kitchen door and crossing the yard joins Amos and Daniel on the lawn. The two men have been looking over the area to determine the best place to build their homes.

"Have you made a decision about where?" she asks them.

"I'll let Amos tell you, Nora. We've been ages discussing blueprints and utility lines and general contractors and even the view! and now I need to get back to my chores." Daniel says with a smile before turning away. Then he stops to add: "He's got some good news as well."

Amos slings his arm across Nora's shoulders and walks her about fifty yards off to start pointing out the area they've chosen to build on.

"We've allocated more land to our plan which gives us plenty of room and that's down to the news Daniel mentioned. We've authorized Luisa to put George down and since we have no other livestock, well... that frees up the paddock."

"Oh! I guess that's good news, I mean it's no secret I hate that old bull with a passion but..."

"But yeah, I know what you mean. It's not really good news or bad news. However, we aren't punishing George we're doing right by him. Luisa said he's now gone completely blind and a bull can't truly function without his eyesight so it's the kind thing to do."

"I guess. It's just... well, the end of something is usually sad news."

"True, but he's outlived the average age and he certainly didn't have a difficult life. I mean George did absolutely nothing day in day out. And the extra land coming available is a silver lining to our housing plans."

"You know Amos I would never have imagined I'd have such a strong nesting instinct," exclaims Nora. "But from the moment you and Daniel started talking about building two homes on the property I can't stop thinking about furniture and bedding and color schemes for curtains and carpet. It's crazy!"

Amos turns a startled face to his new bride. He's uncharacteristically at a loss for words and just gapes at her.

"What? Why are you looking like that?"

In a hoarse voice barely above a whisper Amos asks: "Nora, are you... are we... having a baby?"

Her dark eyes widen comically and her expression is equally as shocked as his own. "No!" she is vehement in denial.

Curious changes flit across Amos's face as his thoughts move from shock to happiness to dismay until he settles on a bland look.

Nora demands to know: "Why would you even think that?"

"Because you're talking about *nesting instincts* which is a reproductive response in animals and humans."

"No, that's not what I meant at all. I'm thinking more along the lines of becoming a homemaker – not that I want to quit work or anything – but, I have this really strong desire to create a comfortable space of our own."

Pulling her into his arms Amos tucks Nora's head under his chin and holds her close. "I like the sound of that: our own place."

Humming happily Nora wraps her arms as far as she can around Amos's waist to hug him back. They stand like that for a pleasant moment when she suddenly says *oh!* and pulls back until she can look him in the eye.

"Amos... would you like me to be pregnant?"

He huffs a bit then gives her a wry smile replying: "Okay I have to admit that for that split-second that I thought you actually were, well... I got really excited over the idea."

"So you wouldn't have minded if.." she doesn't complete the sentence and Amos hurries to answer: "No, I would... huh! I would have been really, really happy Nora."

"Amos! I had no idea."

"I guess I just had an epiphany when I thought... but Nora we've always discussed having children as some far-off thing so I don't expect that to change. I know you love your job and we're just getting settled into married life and—"

"Yes!" she interrupts, then stops. She bites her lip as if holding back words and her eyes are suddenly shining with tears.

Amos takes hold of both her upper arms and rubbing up and down searches her face for clues. "Nora, my love! Nora, what are you saying?"

The tears spill down her cheeks only to get caught in her wide grin. "I'm saying *yes! I'm ready*. Amos I would love to start our family now."

Laughing he crushes her to his chest before capturing her mouth in a passionate and emotional kiss. Her tears leave a salty taste on her lips and he murmurs *I love you! I love you! I love you!*

Advice Given

Milly can't stop her eyes from straying to the wall-clock when Janice Peart enters the farm shop. It's two-forty and they close at three in the winter-time. The days are short with the sun setting before five and Sweet Berry Cove doesn't have street lighting. There's no need for it since the farmers are early risers meaning few people are out and about in the evenings.

Of course Janice notices Milly's glance and she purses her lips in a prim line of disapproval. Miz Tally comes in behind her neighbor and Milly's smile at the old lady, one of her favorite people, is genuine. Milly secretly thinks of her as *my fairy godmother*.

"Milly! Why the long face? I promise we'll let you get away before early closing–"

"Oh no, that's not a problem at all Miz Tally. You take your time, I'm in no rush."

"Hmm, then it's something else that's got you moping," declares Janice.

Shaking her head Milly begins: "It's nothing, really–"

Gently interrupting the girl the older lady comes closer saying: "Obviously it's something, my dear."

"No really, it's silly... it's just me being silly."

Janice snorts in agreement to the likelihood of that, but the kindness in Miz Tally's eyes convinces Milly to confide her thoughts.

She hesitates only a moment before blurting out: "It's Daniel, he's acting like... well, he's treating me like we're already married yet we've never actually dated or anything. I mean, not really... and it's been weeks."

Hiding a smile at the drama of youth Miz Tally nods stating: "Hmm, it sounds like you feel something is missing, something has been left out. Aha! you want to be wooed, that's it, isn't it?"

Blushing Milly looks away and mumbles: "Oh forget about it... I said it was silly."

"No, that's not silly, but the way you're being now certainly is. Why shouldn't you be wooed and pursued? What you want from Daniel is the most natural thing in the world."

Surprisingly Janice intervenes in support insisting: "Don't you let that Daniel Young take you for granted, missy. He's a good-looking bachelor and he knows it. Don't make things too easy for him. Make him sit up and take notice."

"She has a point, Milly. If you say nothing then nothing will change," the elderly woman gently chides her. "You can't expect Daniel to read your mind... delightful as that notion might be! Men sometimes need a bit of a push."

"That's what got me in this pickle in the first place!" Milly retorts then squeezes her eyes shut whispering: "Please pretend you didn't hear that," but she knows that's a hopeless plea when she's skewered by a look from Janice Peart.

"You're going to have to explain that remark," she quickly insists.

Miz Tally lays a hand on Janice's arm before assuring Milly that: "You don't have to say anything you don't want to."

Milly's first reaction is to keep her business private and she's grateful for the out Miz Tally has given her. She presses her lips tightly together, but

14

it's no use. She's compelled by the benevolent look in those faded blue eyes to open her heart.

The whole story comes out, from eavesdropping on the brothers' conversation to her own little game with the dog. By time she's done the old lady's eyes are twinkling with merriment and she's barely suppressing a chuckle. *Even that Janice Peart is smiling!* Milly notices.

The girl looks sheepish at her admission but her demeanor simply adds to her appeal.

"My dear my advice is to let Daniel know what you want."

"Oh, but I couldn't just come right out and say *romance me*. That would be so awkward!"

"No, I see that, but... hmm, how about steering the conversation that way at the dinner table?"

"How do you mean?"

"Let me think. Janice help me out here, I—oh, I know! you could ask Samuel to tell you about Ruth. Mention we were in the shop and her name came up in passing and you realized you know next-to-nothing about her. It's natural you'd be interested in Daniel's mother. You could ask how they met, how he proposed to her, something like that."

Janice remarks: "And if I know Amos Young he'll jump into the conversation to talk about himself and Nora and how he won her over."

Milly's cheeks turn a pretty shade of pink and her eyes sparkle with excitement listening to the two women's ideas.

"That's good advice! I can definitely do that. Oh yes, oh thank you, thank you so much!"

"Well just make sure you let us know how it turns out," Miz Tally's eyes are positively bright now, while Janice's look greedy for gossip - as usual!

Nevertheless Milly promises *I will, for sure!*

Glancing around the Farm Shop Miz Tally explains: "Milly, we actually came to see what's on offer for Christmas. Do you have a flyer printed?"

"I don't, sorry! I'll post something on the home page of the webstore tonight and print off some copies for you."

"No need for that, my great-nephew has me set up on an iPad. It's very convenient for him and his sisters to keep in touch with emails but oh! I forgot, I don't have the Internet."

Milly is about to explain that email uses the Internet but stops herself in time. Obviously these relations want to keep Miz Tally safe from any scams and other nasty stuff that floods the World Wide Web.

"No problem. Give me your email address and I'll send you the website link, all you have to do is click on it. As a rule you shouldn't click links in emails but I promise my site is perfectly safe."

"Oh I'm sure it is dear. My email address is quite long, though. It's my full name, Tallulah Beaumont, but with no space in between my first and last names, then that funny @ symbol then, again no space, gmail.com. Oh and no capital letters either."

Milly writes out *tallulahbeaumont@gmail.com* and showing the note to Miz Tally asks: "Is this right?"

"Yes that's it exactly. How clever you are, Milly."

"No, no, it's you, you were very clear. Anyhow, I've got it. And Mrs. Peart you're already on the shop's email list so you'll get the flyer as well."

"Hmmph, yes. I had to sign up in order to get that special offer, you know when you first opened up the webshop. You should do another one of those, giving discounts is a good way to get more business."

"Not that you'll have any trouble finding customers, Milly. Your Thanksgiving food gifts were so prettily wrapped up and everyone enjoyed them so much, saying they were simply delicious."

"Well I'm glad to hear you say that Miz Tally because it's gonna be pretty much the same thing for Christmas except with Christmassy ribbons and colors. Plus gingerbread, shortbread, and fruit cake. Oh and those individually decorated cupcakes that were so popular at Thanksgiving with the choice of pumpkin spice, carrot cake, and chocolate."

"You didn't mention fruit cake," complains Janice.

"Oh fruit cake for sure! I've done a bit of promotion for our exclusive Sweet Berry Cove fruit cake. Anyone can follow the recipe, but they need to use ingredients from The Cove to get that authentic taste."

"My mouth is watering already!" chuckles the old lady. Turning to Janice Peart she lets the younger woman take her by the arm as they leave the shop calling out their good-byes.

Milly sees that it's now three-ten and considers herself lucky.

Helena Visits Samuel

Unable to settle at home Helena Larch decides to visit Samuel Young right away. Looking up at the front door she has second thoughts about calling on him after all this time. She hesitates to move forward and knock, suddenly regretting the impulse driven by Reverend Smithson's urging and assurances.

This place holds so many memories from when she was a child right up until when she moved away from Sweet Berry Cove. She reminds herself that they're good memories.

A dog barks loudly at her footsteps on the stairs. When the door opens and Samuel greets her with a big smile Helena bursts into tears. The older man immediately welcomes her in with a comforting *oh poor child,* and Helena allows herself to be drawn inside.

Offering refreshment that she waves off Samuel turns away from the kitchen and takes her to the sitting room for privacy. Seating the two of them on the sofa he takes her hand and rubs warmth into it. Helena dashes tears from her cheek with her free hand thinking *I came here to talk, the crying can come later.*

"It's been a long time since you visited me, plenty of changes in your life, but other than the tears you are looking well, my dear. Maybe a little too thin, a little pale, but still a very beautiful young lady."

"Oh Mr. Young–"

"Uh-uh, none of that. You've always called me Samuel."

Helena gives a deep, relieved sigh. It feels like the years have fallen away and she's once again the teenager who spent a lot of time at this farmhouse, relaxed and happy, talking to the man she's always considered to be a second father.

"You're right, Samuel. A lot has happened," she pauses, looking at him helplessly. "I don't know where to start–"

"How about I tell you what I know and then you can catch me up?" At her nod he continues: "Your whirlwind romance was the talk of the town. You and your husband moved away but recently you returned to Sweet Berry Cove. Alone."

Helena still doesn't speak but once again her eyes fill with tears. Samuel squeezes her hand and gently asks: "Do you want to tell me about it?"

With a gulp she nods vigorously until a loud hiccup makes them both smile. "I do, I need your wisdom."

"Oh my dear, I've never been more than a sounding-board to bounce your own ideas off of. You've already got the answer inside you, I'm just here to help you navigate your way to it."

"Well... the first issue is money. You know we've been poor ever since Dad died. Maybe before, too, but I never knew about that. However, once it was just me and Mom it was obvious.

When Chris, my husband, came into my life he swept me off my feet. I was sick and tired of penny-pinching and making-do and settling for less, you know? He's so handsome, too, and he offered glamor and wealth. Best of all he was crazy about me. Everything was perfect well... his income did fluctuate, he does something with investments, but mostly there was plenty of money.

We have a nice apartment, a condo, with both our names on the title. He's got a really nice car and I'm taking driving lessons so that I can get a car, too. We go out for dinner and to the movies, to the horse races, and dancing all the time."

"Sounds wonderful," Samuel remarks.

"It is... it was, but then... oh, I don't know. It's hard to explain..."

"Just say the words like you're telling me somebody else's story. I won't interrupt or comment until you finish."

Straightening her spine Helena gives a decisive nod and relates an unusual tale.

"One day Chris got a phone-call on our land-line which is a rare thing so I listened because I was curious. I watched his face turn white while listening to whatever was being said. He just stared, not blinking even, before he fell into a chair and still he hadn't said a word beyond *Hello?* I was really starting to worry, I'd never seen him like this. Then he said *give me your phone number* and he jotted it down then he ended the call saying *I'll get back to you asap.*

By now I was by his side, rubbing his shoulder and asking *what's wrong? what's happening?* and at first he wouldn't answer but then... then he said, and I'll never forget it, he spoke in a kinda monotone voice like he was in shock or something. He said *my ex is... gone... she's died, and my daughter needs me. I need to step up and be her Dad.*"

She breaks off there and Samuel's heart grieves for the stunned, broken look on her face. He patiently waits for her to gather herself together to go on. When she does her voice is a harsh whisper.

"I never knew he had a daughter, or an ex. I had to leave. I mean, once I found out he had another family... he might not even be my husband! Maybe he's a bigamist and we were never legally married? What then?

Oh it's too shameful." She chokes over the words and takes a moment to compose herself.

"When I said *what are you talking about?* he said *I don't know I don't know anything about her... I have to go find out.* Well that made no sense, I mean how could he not know?

He went into our bedroom and packed a suitcase. I stood in the doorway watching, I couldn't think of thing to say, but when he tried to kiss me goodbye I turned my head. That's when he assured me *everything will be okay,* and he left."

"So he went to...?"

"West Virginia, he said when he phoned."

"Okay, he must have flown since West Virginia is across the country, and what did he find out when he got there?"

"I'm not sure. He called saying he was with his daughter and her aunt had come to stay with her but only until he showed up. So I said, *you never told me you'd been married before* and that's when he tells me he wasn't.

Apparently he'd had a relationship with this woman Melanie, *just a fling* he called it, and after he moved on she discovered she was pregnant. But she never told him. She gave birth to a girl, named her Amelia, and raised her on her own. He never even knew this girl existed, never even knew he had a daughter."

"Ah, so now the girl's mother has died?"

"Yes, she's dead. I didn't ask what happened. This woman, Melanie, has a sister and she's the one who got in touch with Chris. The girl, Amelia, is being looked after by this aunt, her mother's only sibling apparently, but she's some professor and doesn't have time to spend raising a teenager. I guess she said *Amelia should be with her father anyhow.*"

"Even though the father is a complete stranger to the girl? Hmmm, my heart goes out to Amelia. She must be feeling totally abandoned and unwanted."

"I guess... but what if she isn't Chris's daughter? I mean, I suppose they can have DNA testing done to be sure."

"Is that what Chris is planning to do?"

"Oh he's convinced she's his. He says she looks exactly like pictures of his mother when she was a girl. Plus he says he can see a resemblance between Amelia and himself. He's certain she's his but..."

"But?"

"I don't know if I believe him about not knowing. How can I stay married to a man I don't trust? I mean, he never said a word about any of this before we got married."

"I see, but then there really wasn't much to say, was there? He'd had an affair and Helena you aren't naive, no doubt there's been more than one. Your husband is a very good-looking man and he was single back then.

I expect you told him about you and Daniel having been engaged – which I'm sure he already knew, this place being what is for gossip. But I don't imagine you went into details, or discussed the other boys who took you out during one of your frequent break-ups, right?"

She sighs deeply and thinks over Samuel's words. Seeing her emotional turmoil he looks at her with a kind expression and taking hold of her other hand as well suggests:

"Stop there for now. You've got a lot off your chest and now it's important to just let yourself feel. Think it all over and I hope when you're ready to talk some more that you'll come back so we can continue."

"Oh I will, I'll come back for sure. Thank you. Thank you so much, Samuel."

Pulling her to her feet Samuel guides her from the room with his arm over her shoulder.

"I'd offer you tea or coffee but I think it's best if you just let everything kind of percolate without any other input or distractions right now."

"You're right, you've always been right—"

"Oh, hardly!" he interrupts with a wry smile.

"I will definitely take up your offer to meet again."

"I'm glad to hear it."

Samuel walks Helena out onto the porch and patting her on the back goes to say something more but Bernie demands their attention. Helena reaches down to scratch behind his ears before saying *thank you, again* and *good bye*. Content, Bernie sits back down at Samuel's feet and the two of them watch the young woman walk away.

He spies his younger son Daniel walking up from the fields. Samuel is ready to call out a greeting but noticing that Milly is walking around the orchard he slips inside the farmhouse to leave the two young lovers alone.

Why is Helena at the Farmhouse?

After her visitors leave Milly does a quick clean-up before putting on her own raincoat. She's ready to head back to the farmhouse, delighted to finish her chores at the Farm Shop earlier then expected even with the interruption.

Fulfilling the orders for Christmas has taken far less time than she spent on Thanksgiving sales. *Of course that's partly 'cause Thanksgiving was a learning experience. It was both mine and the online store's first holiday and since then I've streamlined a lot of my processes. That's made Christmas easier*, she thinks with satisfaction.

She doesn't mind Miz Tally dropping by. *It was especially nice of her to pass on those compliments. She always makes me feel good. I'll have time to update the website before dinner and can send her the link. To her iPad! good for her for trying new technology.*

The Young's Family Farm Webstore has been a success from Day One. Milly put in a lot of hard work to get it set up with assistance from Nora and Esther, the two sisters-in-law, and support from the men in the family. Her plan to expand the physical store to include a small café will launch in the new year.

She and Daniel discussed what they'd need and Milly found the list daunting. Thankfully Daniel and Amos spent the month of November working through all the requirements. They had to order a dishwasher, freezer, glass-fronted cooler, tables and chairs, plus the tableware. In addition they needed a health permit and were required to install another sink and fire extinguishers in order to pass the inspection.

The family decided to get through the busy Christmas season before launching the new venture so the furniture is stacked in the storeroom waiting.

Looking out at the muddy path Milly turns back to the counter and writes herself a note to order a mop and bucket to keep the floor clean. Prior to Milly's arrival the Farm Shop didn't open year-round so all they ever needed was a broom for sweeping.

Locking the door she pulls up the hood of her jacket. The rain has stopped but the air is misty and moist enough to frizz her brunette locks. Milly's natural beauty doesn't require much maintenance but she does fuss about keeping her hair smooth. Despite using both conditioner and leave-in conditioner any dampness makes her ends curl haphazardly.

Naturally she longs for dead-straight hair since it's common to want the opposite of what we have.

She likes Miz Tally's suggestion to introduce the topic of romance and proposals into the dinner conversation. She hopes Daniel will be inspired by the love stories of his father and brother and thinks *fingers crossed! this just might work.*

The farmhouse isn't far away but the walk is long enough to give her legs a good stretch. Soon she's striding with arms swinging and enjoying the exercise and freshness of the after-rain air. Rainy days are typical winter weather here.

Same as oh! I was going to say home, she muses, *but no, Sweet Berry Cove is my home now. I've lived here for four months and they say it only takes three to adapt.*

With her brighter mood coloring her viewpoint she decides the winterized farm is sleeping, protected against the cold, rather than being the desolate and deserted place depicted by her early morning misery.

She can glimpse the roof of the farmhouse but the front is hidden by apple trees. The path skirts around the orchard and Milly spots a bright blue coat as someone, a female, walks away. Milly can't be certain from just the back-view and at this distance, but she's pretty sure that blonde hair belongs to Helena Larch. She remembers noticing the wearer of that coat just the other day and *yes, it is Helena,* she decides.

Milly is mildly curious about why Helena would be at the farmhouse. She was able to observe Daniel's reaction first-hand that time Helena dropped in on them at the Farm Shop. He didn't act particularly friendly towards his ex. *Hmm, his ex who has come back again and is living with her mother not her husband.* That thought pops up from nowhere and Milly is slightly disturbed by it. It niggles at the edge of consciousness but she pushes it down deep.

Right now her mind is too taken up with thoughts of her little café and the jaw-dropping amount of money it cost to set up. That just adds another concern to her worries. She fervently hopes to realize enough profit to make the Young's investment worthwhile.

No one is complaining, or pressuring her, but Milly is conscious that this venture of hers has been backed purely on good faith. She's determined to make a go of it.

Once she's clear of the last tree Milly can clearly see the front porch. Daniel stands on the steps looking her way and smiling. Milly happily waves and Bernie, their huge Saint Bernard puppy, comes bounding over to hurry her homeward.

The sight of Daniel's grin, his dark good looks and strong, well-built physique sends butterflies fluttering in her tummy. Sometimes it's hard to believe such a handsome man is her boyfriend. *Boyfriend is the wrong word for him,* she thinks. *Daniel is a grown man... fiancé sounds much better, even if he hasn't actually asked me to marry him yet.*

As Milly draws closer Daniel admires how water droplets sparkle in her wavy hair and add a dewiness to her pink complexion. Milly's fleeting thought, wondering what Helena wanted, comes and goes as Daniel pulls her into his arms for a proper greeting.

Their lips press together gently and then more passionately as they both get lost in kissing each other. This is exactly the kind of kissing she's longed to experience. Daniel hums with satisfaction as Milly melts in his embrace with a blissful sigh. The two of them like this is what she wants.

She'd prefer to hear the actual words, but she's happy to accept any demonstration of affection. Any sign that he finds her attractive, maybe even pretty, and hopefully lovable.

Marriage Proposals

While preparing supper for the family Milly mulls over what she hopes to accomplish, and then rehearses the words she will use to achieve this. This makes her feel very organized and clever, and the planning calms her nerves.

It helps boost her confidence when she's competently organizing a meal, comfortable in her own milieu. The farmhouse kitchen is a haven of warmth and color, aromatic and welcoming.

And Milly feels encouraged by the passionate kiss Daniel gave her just before they came inside.

Now that she's seated at the dinner table and faced with the actual conversation well... *it's one thing to imagine what people's responses will be, but quite another in real life,* she thinks.

Clearing her throat she begins: "Samuel, Miz Tally was in the Farm Shop this afternoon and in the middle of our conversation she mentioned your wife. I asked about her and Miz Tally said she really liked Ruth but told me to ask you, saying you two had a real love affair.

She told me some of that before, and you and I talked about it then, but I know there's plenty more to learn."

Samuel puts down his knife and fork, leans back in his chair, and smiles widely at Milly. "My dear you picked my favorite subject! I love talking about Ruth. She was such a wonderful woman. Kind and smart and capable in everything she did.

Not perfect, of course, in fact she was well-known to have a temper and a sarcastic way with words. It was funny if you weren't her target, but if you were, oh boy your ears would burn with embarrassment."

He chuckles at a memory and Amos joins in adding: "I was usually her victim! and Dad's right, Mom let you have real zingers. Thinking back now some of what she said was downright hilarious, but when it was happening, hmmph," he breaks off abruptly, shaking his head.

Daniel's mouth twitches into a half-smile as he obviously remembers something – probably at Amos's expense – but he keeps on eating and doesn't comment.

"Dad," whines Esther, "Milly said Miz Tally told her you had a real love affair so tell us about that. I don't have enough memories of Mommy."

Reaching for his daughter's hand Samuel gives it a squeeze before agreeing that Esther was very young when Ruth passed. Thinking a moment he asks: "You heard the story of how we met, right?"

"Maybe... but I don't remember," the girl fibs with a pout that instantly wins her father over.

"Oh well then, here goes. I was studying Agricultural Engineering at CalPoly when a professor invited *anyone who is interested* to Sweet Berry Cove for a barn-raising. I'd never heard of the place but this was a real opportunity to see how the whole community comes together to help their fellow farmers. And I was young so when he added that *afterwards they have a dance planned* I was all in."

"That's right, I remember Mom saying you two met at a dance," puts in Daniel.

"I fell in love with your mother at the dance but I met her during the day when she worked right alongside me." Samuel's eyes take on a dreamy look as his thoughts drift far back in time.

Speaking slowly he continues: "It was hot, real hot, that day and Ruth's face was pink from sunburn and damp – shiny – with sweat. She'd have hated that if she realized but I just thought she looked so bright and fresh.

I took off my shirt, I had a vest on underneath of course, but I still spotted Ruth casting these sneaky glances my way," he stops and chuckles, "I made sure to flex my muscles with every movement, showing off as young men do."

Amos and Daniel burst into loud laughter while their father gives them a mock glare.

"That's hysterical!" declares Amos.

"Hey I wasn't the only one. Your mother, like most of the women, wore loose cotton pants and as the day wore on she rolled them up higher and higher until I could hardly take my eyes off her legs. It's a miracle I didn't smash my thumb with the hammer I was so distracted!"

"Oh Daniel would definitely have injured himself, he's been a real disaster-magnet lately."

Nora gives her husband an arch look before casting her eyes at Milly and saying: "Not so much anymore though..." and Daniel gives her a wry smile.

"So you two fell in love and got married and just stayed here forever after," Esther says to clarify things.

"That's right, sweetheart. This was the Johansen farm, your mother's family, who owned the land going back several generations. Ruth never wanted to live anywhere else. It was a dream come true for me because not only did I get to marry the woman I loved but she came with a job attached. Two lifetime commitments and I couldn't have been happier."

"Did you have to ask her father for permission to marry his daughter?" asks Milly, trying to draw the talk back to her original script.

"Oh that was funny. I was all prepared to ask Mr. Johansen for Ruth's hand which was pretty nervy when you figure I didn't have any real prospects yet, still being at University. I'd been invited for supper and planned to speak with him after the meal, but instead he asked me flat out at the dinner table what my intentions were."

"Really?" squeals Nora, "This is starting to sound like an old-fashioned novel!"

"And way to single you out, huh?" agrees Amos.

"I was flummoxed. I mean, I was pretty sure Ruth felt the same, but not a hundred percent sure, and you're right he really put me on the spot.

Everyone round the table, the staff always ate with the family, just stopped eating and looked at me expectantly. Except Ruth. She just stared down at her plate either embarrassed by her father or anxious about my answer. I never knew which, but seeing her looking like that uncertain and cowed, did something for my courage.

No way was anyone going to shame my Ruth so I spoke up and told him *it's my heart's desire to marry Ruth, and I believe it's her heart's desire to keep living here, so if that's what she wants, and if she's willing to have me, then that's what I intend to do.* I was speaking to him but I was staring at her. Well, at the top of her head 'cause that's all I could see."

"Good for you, Dad," states Amos.

"Thinking about it now I'm sure I sounded pretty arrogant but I meant what I said and when Ruth finally looked up to meet my eyes hers so full of happiness I knew I'd done the right thing."

"But... you never did actually propose to Ruth, did you?" asks Milly.

Samuel tilts his head and casts his eyes up in thought before replying: "No, I never did. Not in so many words. Mr. Johansen just kind of grunted and gave me a nod while Mrs. Johansen was all smiles and happy tears.

Ruth cocked an eyebrow at me and said *you shouldn't let my father back you into a corner, Samuel.* And me, still feeling brave and proud, told her *I love you with every bit of my heart, Ruth Johansen, and I'll be a good husband to you.* I didn't care who heard me, as it happens I wanted them all to hear.

Ruth's eyes got all shiny with unshed tears and her lips were trembling, I was wishing we were alone so I could kiss her, and she answered *I'll see that you are!* and that broke the tension from all that emotion and everyone toasted and congratulated us."

Esther gives a happy sigh then turning to Amos asks, "What about you? Did you ever actually propose to Nora?"

Milly is delighted with the way the conversation is flowing naturally. *Surely it will get Daniel thinking and maybe this is just the push he needs,* she hopes.

"Of course I did, nosey girl. I proposed on our first date and every date thereafter until I wore her down and she finally said yes."

"Actually that's how you asked me out for the first time. You said, and I quote, *you're going to marry me eventually Nora Perez, so come out to dinner with me tonight and we can start getting to know each other.*"

"That's right! I'd forgotten that. See, I knew from the moment I laid eyes on you that you were the only one for me."

"Love at first sight?" jeers a heavily skeptical Daniel.

"Yeah it was. Well, it was for me. I know you're going to say I only fell for her pretty face but no, I knew right then and there that some day I'd make Nora my wife."

"And Esther it really is true that he asked me to marry him on every single date we had – and every phone conversation, too! Finally one day I was so exasperated I put him to the test. See, I wasn't sure if it was just a come-on line, you know, so I decided the next time Amos asked I would say *yes, I will* and then I'd find out if he was all talk or what."

Stretching his long arm to reach around his wife's shoulders Amos pulls Nora close and giving her a quick kiss says: "You sure did find out, didn't you?"

Nora laughs as she explains Amos let out the loudest whooping cheer, picked her up and spun her round and round yelling *she finally said yes! we're getting married!*

Everyone joins in her laughter at the picture she's just painted for them.

Turning to her other brother Esther declares: "So now it's your turn, Daniel."

Milly senses the sudden stillness in Daniel and she looks down at her plate with just the tiniest hint of a smile on her lips. *Here is comes!* she thinks, desperately fighting the blush she feels rising. Until Esther shatters her peace by adding: "How did it happen when you proposed to Helena? What did you say?"

"Esther!" exclaims Samuel, followed by Amos shaking his head at his sister while Nora explains: "That's not a very tactful subject, is it Esther? It's all in the past."

Stung by their disapproval the girl retorts: "That's why I asked! because it *is* old stuff that happened long ago so it's okay to talk about it now. It's not new like things are with Milly."

"It's still inappropriate—" begins Nora but Milly, determined not to give a hint of what she's feeling, starts picking up plates as she stands saying: "That's enough of that topic, who's ready for dessert?"

She's disappointed when Daniel doesn't speak up. Not trusting herself to look in his direction she holds the tears burning behind her eyes at bay, promising herself a good cry into her pillow tonight.

As usual Milly's dessert is warmly received with plenty of praise but Daniel is preoccupied and doesn't say anything. The moment he's scraped up the last bit of apple pie with sweet cream his chair is pushed back and he leaves without a word. A minute later they can hear him call to Bernie for *walkies.*

Still preoccupied, Daniel is nearly bowled over in the dog's excited rush. Once they're outside the house Daniel continues puzzling over the dinner conversation. Something's off, but he can't figure it out. He's replaying the words trying to identify the sour note. Esther bringing up Helena of all people didn't help... but no, that's not it.

Frustrated he exhales so loudly Bernie turns back with a questioning look. Daniel can't help smiling at the dog whose face is so expressive it's like he's actually speaking.

"Yeah buddy, I don't know why but I can't shake this feeling that I've screwed up somehow. Dad and then Amos and Nora were reminiscing, but I had no memories to share so why do I feel like I've come up short? I mean, I'm not going to talk just for sake of hearing my own voice, right?"

Bernie woofs as if agreeing and when he doesn't hear sadness or anger in his master's tone he happily bounds away again. Daniel is left puzzling over his thoughts.

Milly follows her usual routine of clearing the table and cleaning up the kitchen. As a rule Nora helps and Esther is supposed to, but the girl constantly comes up with a reason to delay or an excuse to get out of it altogether. The older women manage better without her grudging help but Milly understands Samuel's purpose in insisting Esther do her share.

Now that school's out and there's no homework emergency Esther reluctantly and slowly carries in just a couple of dishes.

Nora chivvies the girl saying: "C'mon Esther, let's speed things up so we can finish quickly."

Milly doesn't bother engaging in the ensuing argument. Ever since the talk about marriage proposals took a nosedive she's been working on autopilot and trying to keep her mind blank. She just wants to get through her chores until she can escape to the privacy of her own room. There she can analyze her thoughts and let her feelings run loose.

Sensing Milly is unhappy, but unwilling to share, Nora respects that and instead stops arguing with Esther in favor of making small-talk about local news from The Cove. It's awkward and even the teenager is affected by the gloomy atmosphere. Guiltily wondering if it's somehow her fault Esther sulks and only grunts in reply to Nora's comments. All three of them are relieved when they can finally turn out the overhead light and go their separate ways.

Reaching her room all Milly wants to do is fall into bed. She doesn't have the pleasantly tired feeling after a busy day but instead suffers the bone-weary exhaustion sadness brings. *I'm no good at plotting and planning, it always backfires on me, I don't know why I bother,* she tells herself. *I don't want to think about any of this, not at all, I just want to sleep.*

Surprisingly she does, but sometime in the wee hours her eyes fly open and she asks aloud: "What on earth was Helena Larch doing here this afternoon with Daniel?"

A Second Visit

It's a subdued group meeting for breakfast. Milly has circles under her eyes and Nora suspects the girl's face, pink from a rough scrubbing with her washcloth, is hiding a trace of tears.

Daniel is cranky and clumsy, cursing when he drops the butter knife and Samuel reprimands him sharply. At least Esther loses her sullen expression when she giggles over Daniel's swearing.

Amos quirks an eyebrow at Nora who shrugs her shoulders indicating she has no idea what's going on and shares his confusion.

No one lingers over their meal today and by time Hannah arrives they've all scattered. She finds Samuel in the sitting-room with the newspaper when she tells him he's got a visitor.

Greeting Helena with a genuinely warm welcome Samuel shows his pleasure at seeing the young woman again so soon. *I hope this means she's ready to make her decision,* he thinks.

Aloud he says: "Will you ask Christopher what he wants to do now–"

Interrupting Helena exclaims: "Oh I already know the answer to that. He wants us to live as a married couple again but with the girl, with Amelia, living with us."

"Ah. I can understand that from his point of view but how do you feel about it?"

Helena's voice drops to a whisper as she replies: "I don't know. I don't even know if I want children of my own! so how can I be a mother to somebody else's child? Except she's not a child, she's sixteen, but she's certainly not a grown-up. Oh! that makes me sound so selfish."

She breaks off in tears but Samuel comforts her by insisting she's got valid concerns. "You have the right to question what the current situation means to you and your future, Helena. It's not selfish to rail against the inequity and even complain *why me?* but at the same time you know you also have a duty to make a choice. *Yes or no*, and only you can decide."

"I realize that Amelia's the one who is really suffering from what happened, with her Mom dying and the big changes in her life, so yeah, I feel like a bad person for complaining about myself."

"No Helena, not at all. You are justifiably worried. Sixteen is a difficult age even without all the extra baggage this poor girl brings with her. It's obvious that Christopher is committed to raising his daughter, and it's wonderful that he's stepping up - as he should - and you say he wants to do that with you by his side?"

Helena nods, unable to answer with words. Tears stream down her face and Samuel wishes there was an easy answer to give her.

Gently he begins: "You're entitled to want to make your own choices Helena, I get that, but unfortunately external circumstances have forced you into a difficult situation."

He makes his next statement with sympathy but firmness. "Only you can make the decision but you must be all-in with your choice. If you can't willingly and wholeheartedly enter into this new configuration of your marriage then it would be best for all three of you to go your separate ways."

"But I love Chris," she wails. "Oh Samuel, what do I do now?"

"Last time we spoke you said you hadn't met Amelia yet, right?"

"No, I found her very existence so difficult to accept that I felt I couldn't face her."

"Because you're angry with her? Or is it in case you develop feelings for her?"

"Well... she's all on her own and Chris is a complete stranger to her. I was trying to imagine how it must be losing your only parent then discovering you have another parent who wants to take charge of your life. I mean, what the heck is this girl going through?"

"See, you're already showing maternal concern."

"No no, I don't think so. Anyone would feel sorry for Amelia, it's only natural."

"Well I think you should meet with her, but before that happens look into your heart and ask yourself one tough question: Do I love Chris and want to stay married to him, no matter what? and if the answer is *no* then I don't think it's fair to involve the girl in your life. But if the answer is *yes* both of you will need all of that love to take the difficult step of rebuilding your marriage with a teenager in the middle of it."

"I really do love Chris, I love him with all my heart," she says earnestly then pauses.

Samuel comments "It sounds like there's a *but* coming at the end of that sentence?"

"Well, it will be more than a bit of difficulty!" she exclaims. "There's all the strangeness of it plus you know how teenagers are and then there's the financial aspect to consider."

"All of that is true but Helena, I've known you all your life and I remember a kind-hearted child who grew up to be a sweet girl and a caring young lady. Ever since your Dad passed away you acted like money was everything to you but I happen to know it's not."

"No, you're right, but the lack of it made losing Dad even worse. Anyhow, I can't ask Chris to choose between me and Amelia because she's still a child and I'm an adult.

I have to make the grown-up decision and.." she stops to gather her thoughts before slowly stating: "I couldn't do something so hurtful to Chris. There is no choice for him, he's the father and has to step up, and I think he really wants to. I should be grateful that my husband is such a good man, I mean all of this really blindsided him too. It's not just me whose world has been turned upside down. All three of us are affected."

"And moving forward will be easier if you can give each other strength, the strength of your love and commitment, to work through the obstacles that you're bound to encounter."

Helena doesn't speak for a few minutes. She's mulling over Samuel's words and her heartfelt reaction to them. Her tears stop and she meets his gaze steadily. With a tremulous smile she nods her head saying: "I want Chris, and I want the two of us to make a happy home for Amelia."

"Good girl!" he commends her. "What's your next step?"

Taking a deep breath Helena sits up straight. "Next step is to tell Chris I want to meet Amelia. Actually, no, first I'll confirm to Chris that I do love him and want to remain his wife, then I'll say I want to meet his daughter. Oh, that's going to be awkward."

"It will, initially, but... I have an idea for something that can make things easier for all of you."

Milly Brings Cookies

Milly is having a fun day at the Farm Shop gift-wrapping the goodies she's baked and bottled. There's Christmas paper with red-and-green plaid ribbons spread over the counter and she's set her phone to play holiday music. Humming along while the printer churns out labels she boxes up the packages for shipping, loving every minute.

In addition to the web shop sales she has a lot of orders to fill locally which keeps her happily busy and earning a profit.

She's on her own today, and there have been no customers since lunch-hour. Lately Daniel has been hanging out at the shop but now that he's almost fully healed there are plenty of chores to catch up on. He and Amos have winterized most of the fruit farm but they still grow produce in the high tunnels.

Making the excuse that *I can't send out these, they aren't perfect* Milly fills a bag with soft ginger cookies. Satisfied with the amount of work she's gotten through today she locks up and heads over to the canvas shelters to surprise Daniel with the treats.

On the way she passes Helena Larch who gives her a subdued hello before hurrying away. There's evidence of tears on Helena's face but she's wearing a small smile now. Millie assumes the young woman met with Daniel and again wonders *what's that all about? and why was she crying?*

Frowning over the incident Milly keeps on walking but her thoughts are all jumbled. *Were those happy tears? or a happy conclusion to sad tears?* Milly then admonishes herself for speculating. *It's a silly waste of time to guess, I'll just ask Daniel straight out.*

Instead of being reassured Milly now worries over the possibility that she won't like his answer. *Oh where is this crazy thinking coming from? I'm not the jealous type and I'm really not insecure... at least I never used to be.* She catches herself scowling and blanks out her negative thoughts to smooth over her features.

Hearing voices at the first high tunnel Milly finds Daniel and Amos manhandling a large fan into place. Straightening up Daniel sees her and grins. Milly's heart skips a beat and she catches her breath at the sight of his handsome face. His smile warms her insides and she feels like the luckiest girl.

Emboldened she mentions passing Helena but just then Amos spots the bag she's carrying and asks: "Is that for us?" He immediately comes forward to open it and inspect the goodies.

"Oh look Daniel, ginger snaps but the soft kind!"

"Hey, don't hog them all," his brother protests, reaching into the bag for himself. He doesn't explain what Helena wanted and Milly forgets all about his ex-girlfriend when he gives her a quick kiss with thanks for the scrumptious cookies.

"These are the rejects–" she begins, but both Amos and Daniel insist *they're divine, but you can offload your rejects on us any time you like* which makes Milly laugh.

"Amos, I'll make you a deal," says Daniel, "If I leave you the rest of the cookies will you finish up here while I walk Milly home?"

Milly is about to protest that she's fine, but instead stops, realizing it will be much nicer to walk arm-in-arm with Daniel. Amos jumps at the chance to have all the cookies to himself. He's glad to see Milly looking her usual self again as he waves the couple off homeward.

They take their time, enjoying the warmth and closeness of each other, and he thanks her again for the cookies.

"I'm so lucky to be getting a wife who can bake the way you do, Milly."

She toys with the idea of asking *why do you assume I'm going to marry you?* but quickly pushes that thought away. She's done trying to manipulate Daniel into saying what she wants to hear. There will be little pleasure and less credence if the words have to be forced out of him. She'll take this moment of compliments and cuddles and call it a win.

Bernie comes bounding over to meet them en route. The puppy can't decide who should pet him first. He darts from one to the other running around their legs with his tongue flying, ears flopping, and yipping happy barks.

Daniel manages to grab hold of the dog's collar and keeps him in place till he calms down. Milly gives Bernie scratches behind the ear and he eagerly licks her hand. Daniel fondly tells him *you're a silly pest* and Bernie barks in agreement.

"He likes when you talk baby-talk to him," Milly points out.

Straightening up to reclaim her arm and continue their walk Daniel explains: "It's called *pet-directed talk* not baby-talk."

Tilting her head back to look up Milly lifts an eyebrow and smirks, stating: "Sure sounds like baby-talk to me."

"That's because you know very little about dog training and really should be reading up on it. Bernie is going to grow into a big animal and it's important that you can control him."

"Aww he's a sweetheart–" she begins but Daniel interrupts.

"True, he has a nice nature but you must be able to make him obey your commands. Soon he'll be strong enough to easily pull away from you if he wants to go tearing after something, and if that something is a skunk or a porcupine he'll get himself in trouble."

"A skunk? Eww, that would be horrible. And porcupines? I've never seen one but I heard they don't really shoot their needles, that's just a myth."

"Quills, and you're right they don't shoot them, but if Bernie attacks and gets a muzzle-full he'll be in agony."

Aghast she cries: "He wouldn't have to be put down, would he?"

"No, no. We could pull the quills out with pliers but he'd be whimpering and shaking the whole time so I'd take him to Doc Bautista to put him under first. Easier on the dog - and us - quicker and less painful. Plus, she'd treat him with antibiotic ointment to prevent infection."

Milly is concerned to hear of the perils a pet can encounter in the countryside and asks Daniel if there's some place nearby where she can take Dog Obedience Training classes.

"I'll teach you myself," he says, adding: "Bernie can learn from both of us at the same time. That way he'll understand he has to obey me and you. Dogs are intelligent creatures who like to learn, it's the owners who have trouble enforcing the lessons," he gives her a pointed look.

Indignantly she declares: "Well I'm not going to hit him!"

"It wouldn't do any good if you did, he's probably already reached the point where a smack from you won't faze him in the least. Bernie wants your approval so patience and a stern voice will do wonders.

Ah, there's Dad waiting on the porch. He's been doing that a lot lately... maybe he feels a bit lonely now that he's retired from most of his duties at the Co-op, what do you think?"

"Oh I think it's just that he misses you and Amos and being around men all the time. Instead he's got Hannah every day plus Esther and Nora now that school's out for the holidays."

But today it's Milly Samuel is waiting for. He begins speaking before they've finished climbing up the stairs saying he has a favor to ask of her. Holding the door open he ushers them inside.

Daniel goes off to wash up but pauses in the hallway when he hears his father tell Milly he's invited some dinner guests.

Daniel comes back asking: "Who's coming over tonight?"

"Not tonight, tomorrow night. They'll be four joining us: Helena, her mother Martha, and her husband Chris along with his teenage daughter Amelia."

Both Daniel and Milly look at Samuel in surprise at his news but he gestures for them to put their things away saying: "I'll explain everything at dinner tonight. Milly if an extra four is too many for you we can order something in."

She assures him four more at the table won't be a problem, but the thunderous look on Daniel's face makes her wonder. Her nebulous fears from earlier return to fill her with unease. *What is Daniel so angry about? and Samuel just mentioned Helena's husband meaning she's still married... and he has a daughter? I'm sure no one ever mentioned that before.*

"Actually, let's make it five and I'll invite Stephen as well."

Daniel grunts, commenting *quite the little party* before stomping off down the hall. Turning to Milly Samuel looks nonplussed for a moment before remembering Daniel's past history with Helena.

"Oh! I didn't think about... but that's such old news and now Daniel has you. A much, much better choice for him."

Milly pats his arm before hurrying upstairs to change out of her work clothes. She hopes Samuel is right about Daniel wanting her, and thinks *what have I let myself in for? it certainly will be quite a party!*

Planning a Dinner Party

Milly's stomach is in knots. Once she's got the dinner served, plates passed around, and everyone eating, Samuel explains his invitation.

"We all heard that Helena Larch was back living at her mother's place. Nobody knew if she'd left her husband or if she was just visiting, but of course there was plenty of Sweet Berry Cove speculation. Anyhow, Helena met with Stephen for some counseling and he suggested she come and talk to me."

Turning to look at the two women he adds: "Neither of you lived here back then so probably don't know that Helena and I were great friends. She definitely saw me as a replacement father figure and I was happy to listen and advise. I was sorry for Martha Hannaford when she lost her husband but it was Helena who I really felt badly about. She idolized Bryce and his death nearly destroyed her."

"I've never met the woman but I've seen her around town," says Nora.

"She came into the Farm Shop. She'd heard about Daniel's run-in with George–"

Daniel interrupts with a *huh!* sound. "She came in because she heard about your windfall, Milly."

Samuel chuckles and nods saying: "Helena was always very money-oriented. Well, Bryce spoiled her rotten. She was used to getting everything she wanted but when he died there was no money at all. Making do and cutting corners made Helena bitter."

Hesitantly Milly says "Well... she did seem very interested in how I was going to spend my inheritance."

"I'm sure she was, Helena was always a greedy girl," states Amos decisively.

"Helena has changed, boys. Her husband, Chris Larch, might have swept her off her feet by throwing money around but apparently he makes a good living and they have a comfortable life. She is deeply in love with him but their marriage has hit a stumbling block that is huge.

I can honestly say you're not going to believe this, it really is incredible, but out of the blue Chris got a phone call that turned their world upside-down. An ex-girlfriend passed away leaving behind a teenage daughter who he supposedly fathered! Helena says he had no idea this girl even existed. He went straight to West Virginia to meet with her, her name's Amelia, and now he insists she's definitely his. He's certainly claiming her as his own."

He pauses to note the wide-eyed stares of his family, each of them gazing at him with rapt attention and faces full of questions.

"Helena's problem is two-fold: first the introduction of a teenager into a childless marriage, and secondly Christopher has lost her trust. She's struggling to believe that he didn't know about the birth. Helena worries that he might have been married before – or still is. She's really having trouble coming to grips with everything."

Samuel stops there. Looking around the table he sees that his audience has gone from hanging on every word to formulating their thoughts into questions. It really is a startling piece of news and everyone was frozen in surprise but now they all begin speaking at once.

"How old is this Amelia?" asks Esther.

Amos doesn't get past: "What a crazy thing to happen!"

Nora recaps stating: "So they got married and were happy together and then she learns he's got a child – a teenager – who is coming to live with them and he didn't know a thing about this girl? I can understand how this revelation would shake the very foundation of their marriage."

Milly simply expresses concern for *poor Helena* and *poor Amelia*.

"Chris and Amelia are staying in a motel just outside SLO. Martha invited them to stay but the Hannaford home is really too small to sleep four people in separate rooms. They're all feeling awkward about the situation, in fact Amelia is meeting Helena and Martha for the first time tomorrow afternoon.

I figured they could come here and we could be like a buffer zone to help them talk to each other through us. The presence of strangers should keep the emotional temperature moderate and being here at the farm will be easier than meeting in a public place."

Daniel speaks for the first time and is somewhat abrupt when he asks: "What are you hoping to accomplish, Dad?"

"I'm hoping Helena will allow herself to hear what her heart is saying. I know you don't have a high opinion of her Daniel, and with good reason son, but she has a kind heart and this young Amelia needs all the kindness she can get."

Nora asks Samuel *who is looking after Amelia now?*

"Helena mentioned an aunt who has stepped in but she actually described herself as an *unwilling in loco parentis.*"

"What's that?" asks Esther.

Nora answers that it's a Latin phrase with legal connotations used when another person represents a child because their parents are unable to do so.

"Yes, Sunshine had to take on that role for me a few times, but for this woman to add the word *unwilling* well, that's just being miserable and nasty," states Milly.

"Apparently she's a professional woman, a professor I think, and made it clear she doesn't have the time or inclination to take on a teenager."

"Oh that's so cold!"

"It seems that way, yes, but Milly this woman obviously chose a career over family. She's already made her decision and accepted the consequences, I don't think we can fault her for that."

"But her own blood!"

"Yes but remember she's Chris's daughter, so his responsibility is far greater."

"That's true, I know. Oh poor girl, she must feel unwanted and inconvenient. How old is she?"

"Helena told me that Amelia is sixteen."

"At least two years away from going to college or making her own way. Yeah, I do feel for the girl," comments Amos.

"She's the same age as me," states Esther, "so she can be my friend."

Samuel smiles at his daughter with approval.

Nora notices that Milly is really concentrating on everything Samuel says, while frowning and showing signs of stress. Nora is puzzled thinking such a reaction over people Milly doesn't even know seems *over the top*. Helping to clear the table Nora gets Milly to confide her concerns.

"I-I can't really say what it is, I just feel anxious. Helena is very beautiful, Nora." Milly makes the statement as if it's an explanation.

"Oh Milly you can't possibly be worried that Daniel might– oh no! that's silly,"

"But what if seeing the two of us side-by-side makes him regret... I mean... oh! what if I don't measure up?"

Taking hold of Milly by the shoulders Nora looks down into the shorter girl's face saying: "I could shake you I'm so annoyed! Milly, Daniel is head-over-heels in love with you. Even if he wasn't, like if he'd never met you, he still wouldn't want Helena. Amos told me Daniel shook off that teenage infatuation years ago. He said it suited Daniel to play the part of gruff bachelor, once bitten twice shy.

Besides, from what Samuel has just told us Helena is deeply in love with her husband. You really are being silly and worrying for nothing. Really. Really and truly."

Milly rapidly blinks back the tears that threaten. She's so grateful for Nora's no-nonsense attitude, it reminds her of her guardian Sunshine's attitude towards life. "But what am I going to feed them?" she asks.

Grabbing the tray loaded with their dessert Nora leads the way back into the dining-room while Milly follows with the coffee pot.

"Milly is fussing over what to serve for dinner so let's have some suggestions," she announces.

"Everything you make is delicious," Amos says earnestly.

"Stew is always a safe bet, don't you think?" puts in Samuel.

"Oh no that's too plain for a dinner party," Milly protests. "But there's not a lot of time to put together something fancy."

Nora has been thinking and now she asks Daniel: "What's your favorite dinner?"

"I really enjoyed that roast chicken with asparagus Milly made two weeks ago."

Laughing Nora replies: "If you still remember that meal from that long ago you must have liked it a lot!"

"Oh but one chicken isn't going to feed eleven people... we'd need three chickens – or a turkey."

Samuel offers to go to the Hutterite farming community and get a fresh bird but Esther complains: "We just had turkey for Thanksgiving and we'll probably have it again at Christmas!"

"Milly, isn't roast beef always a safe bet? asks Amos.

Smiling Milly nods saying yes and she's already got a few roasts in the freezer. "I'll need at least eight pounds, no better make it ten. I'll take a roast out to defrost. Thank you Amos, that's a great idea."

"Oh you can be sure that my husband will always suggest beef over poultry any day!" laughs Nora.

After the coffee cups and dessert plates are cleared away Daniel follows Milly into the pantry. There are two freezers, a chest and an upright, against the back wall and he frowns as he watches Milly busily sort through neatly labelled packets. Satisfied with what she's found Milly turns and seeing Daniel standing in the way gives him a questioning look.

"Milly I don't want you fussing over this meal. Dad shouldn't have just sprung this on you–"

"Oh I don't mind, Daniel. Samuel has done so much for me I'm happy to help him out."

"That's nice of you, but you're really busy at the Farm Shop now and Christmas is coming right up so it doesn't seem fair to land you with a crowd for dinner."

Smiling Milly lays her hand on Daniel's chest as she assures him cooking for five guests is fine, but she appreciates his concern. He takes hold of her hand and pulls her in for a kiss. When their lips lock together neither one can hold a thought in their heads.

Reverend Smithson Talks

I'm a real clock-watcher today, sighs Milly as she glances up at the wall to check the time once more.

She prepped what she could for tonight's dinner before leaving the farmhouse this morning. The roast is marinating with root vegetables and Hannah promised to put it in a low oven at 2 o'clock. Dinner is for 7:00 which gives everyone time to wash up after their day's work and head over to the Young farm.

Just as Milly decides to close up a bit early the tinkle of the bell announces a customer. Her heart sinks at the sight of the middle-aged busybody.

Typical of that Janice Peart coming in right near closing time, Milly thinks. *She knows the Farm Shop shuts early in the winter. Well I can't let on that I'm in a rush or she'll dawdle on purpose.*

"Good afternoon, Mrs. Peart. It's a change to see you out shopping on your own."

"Miz Tally is feeling a bit poorly. She thinks she's coming down with a cold *and no wonder,* I told her, *with your nieces and nephews coming round with their youngsters all the time.* Children are just walking germ factories and these people should realize they're putting an old lady at risk. But no, they think of nobody but themselves. It's convenient for them to drag their kids around and that's just what they do." She finishes with a decisive nod.

Milly responds saying: "Oh no, really?" That expression, along with *it's hard to believe, fancy that,* and *how difficult for you* are her chosen stock responses to Janice Peart's tirades.

"Yes, really. It's a disgrace and I've told Tally that to her face. Anyhow, I thought I'd get some of your chicken stock and feed her a nice bowl of hot broth."

"Oh that's very thoughtful of you, Mrs. Peart."

Janice preens, accepting the praise as her due. Still, she takes whatever advantage she can get saying: "Seeing as it's for Miz Tally, and since she gets a discount here, I think I should pay her price for this purchase."

Milly bites the inside of her cheek to keep from smiling. She was going to give the soup container to Janice for free but not now. Now she sighs deeply before capitulating and the older woman smirks with satisfaction.

"You're not very busy today, are you?"

"No, not at all. I was actually thinking of closing a bit early."

"You'd have missed my sale if you'd done that. You're lucky I came by when I did. At least you had one paying customer in today and–" before Janice can finish the bell tinkles again and both women look to the door to see Reverend Stephen Smithson enter. He greets them with a big smile as he comes up to the counter.

"Good afternoon, ladies. It's a chilly day but at least the sun's shining." Looking out the window he adds, "For another hour or so that is."

"I wouldn't say it's chilly," argues Janice Peart. "The air is brisk. It's healthy and bracing." She straightens her posture and lifts her chin. Milly has an image of Janice Peart marching down the road counting *hup, two, three, four* under her breath.

"You're absolutely correct Janice, it does feel invigorating." Turning back to the counter he admires the display of baked goods before delightedly pointing and exclaiming: "I haven't seen an old-fashioned cinnamon sugar donut in I don't know how long. Seems nowadays they've all got cream or custard or jam inside them. Oh Milly, I definitely need to buy half-a-dozen– no, better not be greedy," He pats his perfectly flat stomach. "I'll treat myself to two of them."

As Milly bags the items and collects the Reverend's money Janice, with an inquisitive tilt to her head, states: "I can't imagine you walked all the way here just to buy a donut, Reverend."

Milly is surprised at such blatant nosiness but the Reverend just chuckles and answers with good grace.

"Actually I came to ask Milly what she does with her leftovers. I mean, I know you have this container marked *half-price from yesterday* which I'm sure the children enjoy, but what happens if these don't sell?"

Before Milly gets the chance to answer Janice speaks over her saying: "Why are you asking about that?"

"Because I thought if these goods end up in the garbage maybe they could be donated. We have both the Senior's Early Supper and the Youth Club Meet-Up each week and a sweet snack always goes over well."

"Hmmph, I suppose that makes sense instead of tossing it out. Maybe you should bake less so you don't have so much left over, Milly."

Milly ignores the implied criticism and mildly replies: "I usually do sellout, though. If I don't I bring whatever is left back home with me."

"Ah, that makes sense. Well I thought it was worth asking and look at the treats I was lucky enough to get!" he beams holding up his bag of two donuts.

"Actually Reverend Smithson which two days do you need desserts? The Farm Shop will happily provide a tray of pastries each week."

"Oh they both meet on the same day, Thursdays, starting at 4:00 for the meal and then the young people come in at 6:00. But you don't have to do that, Milly–" he begins.

Milly interrupts saying: "I'm happy to, maybe it will attract some new customers." Chuckling she quips: "You know recommendations by *word of mouth,* literally!"

"I'll be sure to credit the source! Now, let's figure this out... you close at 3:00 in the winter so I'll plan to send someone round to pick up at... what time?"

"I'll have it ready by 2:30 to give you a bit of leeway."

"Well this is very kind of you, Milly."

"Hmmph, kind of Samuel Young I'd say since it's his business," puts in Janice.

"That's right," agrees Milly, "and we all know how kind-hearted Samuel is."

"I'll thank him in person when I see you all tonight. Oh! I'm sorry to have kept you late, Milly. I'm sure you've got plenty to do to get ready for the dinner party," he apologizes.

Janice Peart's nose actually twitches now that she's been alerted to *news of something happening in The Cove.* She's eager to know all the details. Gallantly extending his arm Stephen Smithson escorts her out the door with the promise to *reveal all.*

Milly flips the door sign to Closed as she locks up behind them marveling at his patience and thinking *better him than me!*

Looking at the clock she shakes her head and hurries to lock the till. *There isn't enough cash to warrant opening the safe*, she decides as she lets herself out the back door onto the path homeward.

Milly Feels Taken For Granted

Hurrying home Milly reviews her tasks. She's worked out a timetable so each of the dishes whether cold or hot, can be served fresh and all together. With that settled in her mind she now considers what clothes to wear.

I'll have an apron on while cooking but over pants or a dress? It's not really a dress-up occasion but every time I've seen Helena I've admired how <u>stylish</u> she looks. Although she's only a few years older than me she's always so poised and put-together... it makes me feel... oh I don't know, less put-together, I guess.

Usually Milly just pulls her long hair back into a low ponytail when working in the kitchen but wonders now if she should style it? *No, it will take far too long to get it curled. I can pull it to one side and braid it to lie over my shoulder. That's a different look without being too fancy. I should probably put on a bit of make-up but what if it smears from the heat of the oven?*

Looking in the mirror as she hangs up her coat she realizes she won't need lipstick having chewed at her bottom lip until it's rosy red. It gives her the idea of wearing something red to feel courageous.

Searching through her closet she finds a red sweater that matches a tartan skirt. Slipping into the clothes she notes that the skirt is quite short and far too young-looking. It feels like she's wearing a school uniform! Changing again, this time into a plain navy a-line, she's pleased with the more mature, business-like look.

Once she's immersed in her cooking Milly forgets all about her appearance.

The Larch family and Martha Hannaford arrive and everyone is standing in the entryway while introductions are made. Reverend Stephen Smithson opens the door calling out a loud greeting. He has a social knack that somehow unites them all into a friendly group just by his presence.

"Right on time!" says Samuel as he directs them straight into the dining-room. Farm families usually dine earlier than this so everyone is ready for the meal.

They're greeted by the sight of a table laden with a big meat platter, serving dishes of sides, salad, *crudités*, and a basket of homemade bread rolls fresh out of the oven. The guests are directed to their seats first, then the family take their usual places.

Nora carries in a couple of gravy boats while Milly follows with Yorkshire Pudding cut into squares and piled high.

Martha Hannaford gives an interested look asking: "What is this?"

"It's Yorkshire Pudding, you've had it before haven't you?"

"Yes, but I've only ever seen it made in muffin tins."

"That's what I said!" laughs Nora.

Milly agrees: "That's the usual way, but I didn't think a dozen would be enough so it's easy to just bake a double batch like a sheet cake and serve it in slices."

Everyone relaxes at the sight and smell of good food, and the feeling of awkwardness passes.

"Everything looks delicious, Milly!" exclaims Amos and they all murmur in agreement. Milly blushes at all the compliments that follow once they start eating.

While the diners search their minds for a topic to begin the conversation the momentary silence is broken by a mournful howl followed by loud barks from Bernie. He's been shut away in the boot room and now he's making sure everyone can hear his plight.

"Sorry about the dog–" Daniel begins but Samuel interrupts telling him to let Bernie out.

"You've trained him not to beg at the table so he'll be fine so long as he can see what's going on. It's the not knowing that bothers him."

"Daniel!" giggles Esther, "Your dog is suffering from *FOMO*!"

At her brother's quizzical look her giggles turn into laughter and Amelia joins her so in unison they shout: "*Fear Of Missing Out*."

Daniel just shakes his head and with a warning plea to everyone that *Bernie will definitely come by for a sniff but please don't feed him anything from the table. I promise he'll get a full dish of beef after we finish.*

Bernie does make a beeline for the guests barely stopping by one set of knees before moving on to the next. Amelia delightfully squeals *isn't he precious!* and her father hooks the dog by his collar to give him a good scratch behind the ears. Bernie is delirious with joy over the company and all this attention.

"He's pretty big, how old is he?" Chris asks.

Daniel answers and hearing his master's voice Bernie hurries over. With a hand gesture Daniel gets the dog to lie down. He knows he won't be fed table scraps but the swiftly wagging tail shows he has no intention of napping.

"Bernie is six months old and he weighs about 90 pounds."

Helena exclaims: "He's only six months? But he's already huge, when will he stop growing?"

"And how big will he get?" puts in Amelia.

"He'll keep growing until he's two and by then he'll have doubled this size."

"You mean 180 pounds of dog?"

Chuckling at Helena's horrified look Daniel quips: "Maybe even 200 pounds."

Casting a fond look at Bernie Samuel remarks: "This overgrown puppy sure is a great conversation starter. Now Helena and Chris why don't you two begin by telling us your plans. Then Amelia I hope you'll feel comfortable enough with us to share what's going on with you. I'm not ignoring you Martha, but you're not a newcomer so..."

"Nope, I'm born and raised right here in The Cove," the older woman replies with a smile.

"I like it here at Sweet Berry," states Chris Larch. "But my job keeps me in the city. Helena and I have a nice place but we're going to need more room so we'll just have to find something even nicer."

"Your condo is great–" says Helena but Chris corrects her saying *our condo*. She gives him a sweet smile before continuing: "But I think it might be time to look for a house, all we need is a bungalow, say with three bedrooms?"

"Maybe four..." her husband suggests and Helena colors up prettily.

Nora has been eager to join the conversation and with her years of teaching skills she quickly puts Amelia at ease, drawing the girl out.

"We're all very sorry to hear about your mother, Amelia. She couldn't have been very old so I'm sure it was a terrible shock for you. Now I think I hear a bit of an accent and somebody mentioned West Virginia?"

Amelia nods in acknowledgement of the sympathy and now says: "Yes, I'm from West Virginia but I don't have an accent, you all do."

The adults chuckle but Esther is quite sincere when she tells the other girl: "No Amelia, you really do have an accent. A Southern accent, although you don't sound as Southern as Miz Tally."

Amos explains to the company that Miz Tally is a senior friend from Georgia who has a real Southern drawl.

"You'll meet her," says Esther, "if you spend any time at all here in the Cove. Her and that Janice Peart go everywhere and know everything about everybody."

Amelia winces but Esther assures her that Miz Tally is nice. With her father listening in she doesn't dare elaborate on Janice Peart.

Nora returns the talk back to Amelia. "What's going to happen with your schooling, Amelia? I realize you won't be going back to school until the new year but where will you be going?"

Amelia shrugs helplessly, casting her eyes to her father. Chris reaches forward to give her hand a squeeze. "Well, I wasn't going to say until I knew for positive but it's 99 percent guaranteed so... I applied for a transfer to San Luis Obispo and I'm hoping we'll relocate there."

"Oh Christopher! that's excellent news. It will be so good to have Helena, to have all of you, near by," says Martha happily.

"Well depending on what part of the city you live in we might be at the same high-school. All of us here in The Cove take the bus to school in town. We got to Saint Catherine's High, which sounds like it's a Catholic school but it's not. It's on the outskirts of SLO."

"SLO?"

"Oh I forgot, you wouldn't know but we all call San Luis Obispo *SLO,* using just the initials, because it's easier to say." The two teens are quite happily interacting with each other.

"I've got to get something arranged about Amelia's schooling right away," Chris says hurriedly. "Helena, we'll have to house-hunt quickly so we know what school district we'll be in."

Nora explains there are at least two dozen public high-schools in SLO and suggests that Amelia be enrolled at Saint Catherine's for now. "I can help you with that, Chris. I'll call Charlene, the school secretary, and find out what information she needs. I expect she'll want to contact your current school to get your grade transcript sent over Amelia, so if you could write down the name and contact info if you have it…"

"I do. It's here in my phone," the girl replies, handing over her phone for Nora to copy down the information.

"After you're done Nora let Amelia text me so we've got each other's numbers," puts in Esther and soon her mobile phone, normally forbidden at the dinner table, is produced to exchange contact info.

"This will be great, I can show you around here and at the school. Today we finished for the holidays so let's meet up tomorrow and I'll give you the Sweet Berry Cove grand tour. We'll go get ice cream and you'll meet everyone there."

"I'm available any time, if it's okay with um, Chris," Amelia answers. She hasn't been able to call him Dad yet but saying Chris doesn't feel right either. It's a bit of discomfiture that everyone chooses to ignore.

"Esther how you can even think of ice cream in December is beyond me," states Samuel.

"Oh I don't know," says Milly, speaking for the first time. "Ice cream always sounds good to me."

Daniel turns to her with a smile saying: "It's that's sweet tooth of yours, that's what makes you so sweet," and Milly blushes at the compliment. It feels like they are few and far between with Daniel. *But that makes them even more special when he does say something nice*, she reasons diplomatically.

"It's her sweet tooth that's pushing me back to the gym to work off all the calories I'm eating every day in cakes and pies and pastries," complains Amos.

Quirking an eyebrow at her husband Nora dryly remarks: "You don't *have* to eat every dessert Milly makes, you know."

With a very serious expression he tells her "No, I really do have to. Everything Milly makes is always so delicious."

"Actually he's right about that, Milly. Even when we're all in our own places you'll still have to do the cooking and baking so we'll keep the farmhouse as the main gathering point for meals," says Nora.

"Oh that sounds good," Samuel enthuses. "I didn't realize you'd decided."

"Yeah pretty much, Daniel and I agreed that we'll build a couple of smaller homes for ourselves with just a few rooms and a second floor for when the children come."

The secretive smile Milly spies on Nora's lips immediately catches her interest and has her speculating.

Stephen joins the discussion saying: "Samuel, I thought you were the one who was going to move into a new smaller place?"

"I was willing, but I like this idea better. From the day I moved in here Ruth and I had such good times and every room is filled with so many happy memories... I can't imagine sleeping anywhere else."

The men elaborate on their plans and it's obvious they've moved on from giving the idea serious consideration to treating it as a *fait accompli*. The information they've acquired about permits, costing, materials, and scheduling is shared with opinions and suggestions amicably discussed.

The diners break into several different conversations and no one notices that Milly isn't participating. She efficiently removes the used plates and returns with re-filled dishes. Her face holds its usual calm expression but inside she feels a hollowness. She resents Daniel deciding on his own where they're going to live.

In fact he's just assuming that we'll be married. Even though he's never actually proposed. Despite all the hinting. She admits to herself that her feelings are hurt at being taken for granted.

But maybe he doesn't realize what he's doing? Miz Tally did say something about not expecting him to be a mind-reader. I should just tell him how this makes me feel but... I don't want to look like a whiny kid. Besides he should know! He's older than me and way more experienced, he's actually been engaged once already so...

Sensing her mood Bernie comes to lay his head on her knee. Bending down she whispers to the dog that his extra dinner will be coming right up. He licks her face making her grin.

Sitting back up she catches Stephen watching her and he gives her a warm smile when their eyes meet. Looking over at Daniel she sees he's noticed the exchange and it makes a blush rise on her cheeks. Stephen never made a secret of his feelings for her but he's nothing more than a friend to both her and Daniel now.

She has no reason to feel guilty and silently curses how easily color floods her face. *Small towns are difficult,* she thinks, *because everybody knows everyone else's business – past and present!*

Helena addresses Milly with thanks for *an absolutely wonderful meal* and soon everyone is passing around compliments. Through it all Milly is very aware that Daniel keeps staring at her. Flustered she rushes into the kitchen to fetch the coffee and desserts. Nora calls out *I'll give you a hand* but it's Daniel's footsteps Milly hears behind her.

Taking hold of her thick braid he lifts it off her shoulder and strokes the plait saying: "This looks pretty. You did a great job, Milly. Dinner was perfect."

Leaning in he kisses her gently then murmurs against her lips *I'm so lucky to have you.*

Nora arrives then so the two break apart. Milly is happy that she's pleased Daniel but can't help wondering if his appreciation is heartfelt or a reaction to Stephen Smithson's admiring look?

Party Hangover

Milly stares into her bedroom closet wondering *why are all my clothes so drab? Nothing stands out, the colors are blah and bland.* Last night she felt like the hired help compared to Helena Larch yet the older girl wasn't wearing anything fancy. But the brilliant blue shade of her blouse was so eye-catching. *She probably wears a lot of blue since it goes so well with her blonde hair and blue eyes.*

And then there was the way she wore her outfit, such confidence! and the clothes themselves were soft, silky fabrics. Everything I own is sensible and serviceable. Garments that will last. Even my shoes are boring. I never owned a pair of high-heels until Nora and Amos's wedding and those are only sandals.

Helena's outfit was perfectly simple: dress slacks and a blouse but the straight leg of her pants ended well above her foot showing off high-heels and a gold ankle bracelet. Effortlessly *chic.* Milly felt frumpy and dowdy despite the brave red color she wore.

But Daniel did compliment my hairstyle, she reminds herself, smiling at the memory. *Still... whenever he looked from me to her he couldn't help but notice the difference between us. He used to love Helena – enough to propose marriage to her – so she's his type and I don't compare... I can't compete.*

She doesn't have time to mope over her wardrobe chiding herself: *I need to just pick something, anything! because I've got to get going. I have breakfast to cook and serve before heading off to open the Farm Shop by 10:00.*

Choosing a pair of navy cords she searches her drawers for a brightly colored sweater but all she finds are pastels. With a heavy sigh she selects a blue mock-turtleneck. Milly doesn't see how the sweater brings out the color of her eyes and the pink of her complexion. The soft wool drapes her curves and the wale of the corduroy makes the material of her pants look velvety. Each of the men look at her with approval as they enter the kitchen for breakfast.

Samuel thanks her again saying: "Milly I truly appreciate all your hard work in preparing that wonderful meal you served to my guests."

Amos agrees that *everything was delicious* then turning to his father adds: "I thought Helena and Chris looked happy together. The arrival of Amelia into their lives must have been a real bombshell, I mean... wow! An unknown daughter and a teenager at that!"

Nora, coming in right behind her husband, opines that *Amelia is a very nice girl, and it seems like she's willing to get along with everyone.*

The three of them continue their discussion but Milly only has eyes for Daniel. He smiles, but it's obvious he's preoccupied with something on his mind.

It's unfortunate that his expression doesn't give her any clues because she'd be delighted if only she could know what he's thinking. Daniel is suffering a bout of jealousy over that look Milly and Stephen Smithson shared. *It was more than friendly... it seemed so cozy, so... intimate,* he thinks, his eyebrows pulled together in a frown.

Milly places the platter of fried ham slices and bowl of scrambled eggs in front of Samuel. He serves himself before passing the dishes on while Nora pours out glasses of fruit juice. A moment later the oven dings with two batches of fresh-baked rolls. Milly brings those to the table and seats herself saying: "I expect Esther will sleep in since it's the first day of her holidays."

"She'll sleep in every day!" exclaims Amos with a laugh. "Oh, to be a teenager again and sleep for eleven to twelve hours at a time."

"Husband, if you can't sleep you must be harboring a guilty conscience," teases Nora.

"If I can't sleep wife," he replies stressing the last word, "then you're to blame."

Nora can't suppress her happy smile but she turns her head and pretends to ignore Amos.

"I thought Esther and Amelia hit it off well, didn't you Samuel?"

"Take the compliment, dear and yes, I agree about the girls. I'm pleased to see it. Esther will love having someone new to show around and hang out with for the next two weeks," her father-in-law answers.

"I know she's got friends at school, but there aren't many teenagers here in the Cove. There's plenty to do outdoors in the winter like hiking and biking, beach volleyball, horseback riding, even whale watching, but you want a friend along for company, especially when you're young."

"I saw some teens at the Hallowe'en Dance and I wondered what the young people do for entertainment here," comments Milly.

"Even though it's colder now they still sit around bonfires toasting S'Mores, sneaking puffs off cigarettes, and probably playing a few kissing games. I know that's what we did when I was in high-school."

"Spin-the-Bottle, huh?" asks Nora archly.

"Oh I'm sure I was just the referee, hon. Help me out here, Daniel."

With a shake of his head Daniel loses his faraway expression and admits he has no idea what anyone's talking about. Nora laughs as Amos complains *some help you are, bro!*

Milly finds she doesn't have much of an appetite. She eats a spoonful of eggs then makes a sandwich of ham-on-a-bun to take with with her to eat at the shop.

When he sees what she's doing Samuel warns: "If anyone catches the aroma of juicy ham in a warm bun they'll be wanting it added to the menu at your café, Milly."

"Don't give her ideas, Dad!" Daniel interjects, "She's got enough on the go as it is."

Daniel's words occupy Milly for the short walk to her work. *Does he think I've taken on more than I can handle with the café?* she worries. *What if the whole venture is a fiasco? They've already spent so much money, what will I do if it's a complete failure? If that happens I'll just have to pay them back.* She arrives at the Farm Shop anxious and fretful.

Daniel Reflects

Daniel can complete his chores without giving them much thought. He finds the routine soothing rather than boring, and he can let his mind wander.

The dinner party went really well. He'd been a bit hesitant, uncertain, about sitting through an entire meal with Helena never mind adding her husband as well, but it was good having the crowd around the family dinner table.

The meal was excellent, thanks to Milly, and the conversation was easy. Amazing, really, under the circumstances.

And I have to say I like Chris Larch, he thinks, recalling their various conversations. *He's a nice guy, friendly, and he likes dogs or at least he likes Bernie, and he obviously loves Helena so... I'm happy for her.*

That's quite a situation they've found themselves in with his daughter suddenly appearing in their lives but Amelia is a nice girl. She's pretty, too, and the three of them look enough alike to blend together as a family.

As usual Helena looked good, but then she always made sure to do so. A picture of feminine perfection from the nail polish on her toes to her expensive haircut. How could I have ever thought she'd settle for being a farmer's wife? Shaking his head he laughs out loud at the foolish arrogance of his younger self.

Helena has been worried and it shows, but I could see her relaxing over the meal. Good food does that, plus Dad is just great with everyone. He always knows what to do and say and he isn't afraid if people get emotional. I wish I had that gift but for me words and feelings... well, they don't come easily.

In his mind's eye Daniel recalls where everyone was sitting around the table and how Helena and Nora were so bright and chatty, how Martha was all smiles, how Amelia was happy to giggle and whisper with Esther who was just as talkative as usual. His Milly was an oasis of calm. Daniel's half-laughing at himself over the fanciful phrase, but it fits.

He can easily remember Milly's face looking interested as her gaze moves from one speaker to another. She nods in encouragement here, chuckles softly there, and when her eyes finds his she give him a gentle smile that brings a satisfying warmth.

Daniel recognized that Milly had made an effort with her appearance. He'd never seen the red sweater that she wore before, but thought it looked really nice on her. For the first time he wonders if she felt anxious about Helena?

After all, she knows we were once engaged... but Helena is definitely not her rival. She wouldn't be even if she wasn't already married. Still, Helena is a beautiful woman, worldly compared to Milly, and there is that history between us so it's possible Milly might have worried.

Perplexed, Daniel is annoyed with himself for not thinking this sooner. *I could have reassured her and smoothed things over. Well, I did tell her I liked the way her hair lay across one shoulder in that thick braid. The twisted strands caught the light showing rich brown and auburn shades.*

Pulled back from one side of her face it exposed the curve of her cheek and her slender neck. Milly shouldn't hide her pretty face behind her hair like she usually does. I can still tell her that, he thinks. Then sourly wonders if Stephen Smithson already has.

He's annoyed about Stephen bullying Milly into providing free treats for his two social clubs. Daniel knows Milly would have volunteered, no guilt-tripping required, but he still resents people constantly piling work on her.

Milly is now responsible for operating the Farm Shop year-round along with keeping the webshop stocked and its website updated. Running the café was her idea but it's still an extra job to add to her growing list.

A list that includes cooking for the family which was only supposed to be breakfast but now is all their meals including dinner parties. And helping to take care of Bernie.

Plus being my girlfriend when she has time, he tells himself suddenly feeling grudging and bitter but not knowing why.

Esther and Amelia get Ice Cream

Chris Larch brought Amelia to the farmhouse in the early afternoon. Esther had finally woken up and sent out a flurry of texts. Now she's happily excited for the two of them to be going out. Amelia is warmly dressed in a sheepskin jacket of Helena's and it looks so good on her Esther can't help but feel a twinge of envy.

The two girls come clattering down the stairs both talking a mile a minute. They're in complete agreement over their favorite girl singers, the best boy bands, their iPhone/Android preference, and everything else they've discussed so far.

"Oh wait!" cries Esther dramatically pausing in mid-step down the stairs. "What about pizza toppings?"

"Well I don't care what anyone says," Amelia declares, "but I LIKE pineapple–"

"YES!" shrieks Esther and the two girls hug before bouncing down to the main floor. Hannah comes out of the sitting-room dragging the canister vacuum like it's a pet and she stops to stare at the teenagers.

"You two know better than to fool around on the stairs," she admonishes.

"Oh Hannah, don't fuss."

"Fine, but when you fall and break your neck don't come running to me!"

The foolishness of that statement has the girls dissolving into helpless giggles and even Hannah can't resist smiling at their joy. Shaking her head she asks *do you want something to eat before you head out?* But Esther says *no, we're going for ice cream in The Cove.*

"Ice cream! In this weather? There's already a bitter cold wind to freeze you on the outside and now you want to chill your insides, too?"

"Well Mrs. Cairns we *are* teenagers..." drawls Amelia, playing up her southern accent.

"Stop I'm gonna pee!" screams Esther laughing hard and jumping up and down.

Hannah throws up her hands at their antics and shrugs at Samuel who has stepped into the hallway to see what all the noise is about. He can't help but chuckle at the sight of the young girls in fits of laughter.

"Do you two want a ride somewhere?" he asks.

"No thanks Dad, but if it's okay I'll call you when it's time to come home?"

"Sure thing, sweetheart. In the meantime bundle up because it will be a cold walk. I expect Amelia will need some winter accessories."

The girls move off to the big hall closet and get themselves outfitted with woolen scarves, hats, and mitts. Esther's bright blue eyes and reddish-brown hair contrast nicely with the off-white fisherman's knits. Light blue sets off Amelia's pale blonde locks and her own ice-blue eyes. Her coloring is so similar to Helena's that they can, and in the future will, be taken for sisters.

Stepping outside Esther shivers stating: "Omigod it's freezing!" She blows out a breath to see the frosty exhale.

"Is it always this cold here?" asks Amelia stomping her feet.

"No, today feels extra cold. But it *is* the third week of December so yeah, I guess this is pretty normal. January is always the worst, and then things start warming up pretty fast."

"Do you get snow?"

"I've never seen it here but further inland there are some ski hills."

"Oh! I wish I could ski. Can you?"

"No... but maybe we can learn together? If we could find someone to take us. The guys from around here don't snow-ski but we all go waterskiing in the summer. Do you waterski?"

"No, but I'd love to try it. Are there many cute guys around here?"

"Huh!" snorts Esther, "more like are there *any* cute guys. But maybe I only think that way because I've known everybody all my life. It's hard to judge, you know?"

Amelia gravely nods and both girls feel wise and mature.

This Tuesday is an exceptionally cold day for the coastal village so the girls don't see many people on their walk. The few who do stop don't stand around chatting for long, just enough to get a good look at *that daughter of Helena's husband.*

Helena's mother Martha arranged with Hannah that the two of them would drop the news about Amelia into casual conversations and between the two of them they've managed to spread the word. Now the whole community knows the outlines of Amelia's interesting story. Some are disapproving and shocked, but most are ready to welcome the girl.

As usually happens opinion is divided over what Helena should do now and what Christopher should have done before. Amelia is a completely unknown factor, but the people who meet her are favorably impressed and pass on approving comments.

Janice Peart is beside herself lamenting to everyone who will listen: "If I'd only known when I was in the Farm Shop yesterday I'd have gotten all the details out of Milly. I should have realized something was up when Reverend Smithson said he'd see her at dinner. I asked *what that was all about?* and he said he'd tell me on the walk home but all he said was Samuel had issued a last-minute invitation to a dinner party. When I asked who else was invited he just said *I expect I'll find out when I get there...* but I bet he knew all along."

Her disgruntled expression doesn't bode well for the Reverend next time she meets up with him, but the man is skilled at deflecting gossip and nosy questions.

Esther and Amelia's late start means they arrive on The Cove's Main Street long after Janice Peart has already gone home. She's stopped in at her neighbor Miz Tally's place and passes on the surprisingly large amount of news she did manage to pick up.

The gossip rallies the old woman for awhile but she quickly slips back into a listless, exhausted state. Using the digital thermometer Miz Tally bought during the Covid-19 scare Janice discovers her friend's temperature is high but not feverish.

"I just need to rest, *to sleep myself better* as my mother used to say." Hearing the frailty of the elderly woman's voice Janice promises to pop in again before bedtime just to double-check. The fact that Miz Tally doesn't argue with this plan, instead thanking her for being such a good friend, worries Janice more than the somewhat high digital readout.

By now the two teenagers have arrived at Sunday's Ice Cream Shoppe. The owner, a fat and friendly woman called Sandy Sunday, is happily quizzing Amelia while the girls agonize over their choice of ice-cream.

"You can mix your scoops if that helps, dear. Now that accent of yours... did I hear you've come from West Virginia?"

"That's right, ma'am. I lived there all my life."

"Ah! and how old are you?"

The shop also sells coffee, tea, and hot chocolate in addition to stocking some of Milly Clarke's baking bought from the Young's Farm Shop. It's common practice for Main Street shoppers to pop in for a drink or a cone while sharing the latest news. Everyone who walks through the door today lingers to overhear Amelia's *Q and A session* with Miz Sandy.

Finally the girls get their order filled and escape to the back corner of the small room. Here their contemporaries have pushed a couple of tables together to hang out. The adults leave them alone although there is some grumbling about those kids hogging all the heat from the fireplace. It's only an electric model but the flames dance and it sends out plenty of heat.

Esther introduces Amelia to the four young people sprawled on the bench seats.

"This is Blaine, that's Audrey, beside her is Joanna, and that guy is Andy."

Smiling and nodding hello Amelia recites to herself Blaine: good-looking blond; Audrey: athletic redhead; Joanna: pretty, but too much make-up; Andy: friendly face, big build.

"Amelia is moving to SLO and will probably be joining us at Saint Catherine's. She's the one whose Dad married Helena Hannaford, you know..."

That news elicits surprised and interested looks. There's no doubt that gossip and rumors about the Larch's marriage have been discussed over every family dinner table.

"Oh wow, that's you huh? Is it true that you never met your Dad before?"

Amelia talked about this very thing with Chris when they got back to their motel last night. Dinner at the Young's farmhouse was supposed to be an ice-breaker and it went really well. No one asked intrusive questions and it was a comfortable evening.

Chris suggested that Amelia brace herself for nosy questions saying *those folks tonight were polite and friendly but not everyone will be. You have to understand that our story will shock a small village and naturally the people you meet will be curious.*

"So what do I say when they ask about us?"

"You go with your feelings, hon. If you don't mind, like if you think the person is nice and genuinely interested, then tell them the truth. But if you're uncomfortable because it's someone being a busybody then look them in the eye and answer right back with your own question: *why do you ask?*"

"Oh! I can't imagine saying something like that, especially not to a grown-up but... it would serve them right! I think I'll have to practice in front of the mirror a few times."

"Well again, remember the small town mind-set so make sure you mean what you say and watch what you do because tongues will wag and memories are long."

Amelia quickly replays last night's conversation in her mind before answering. She doesn't detect anything spiteful or nasty in Andy's voice so she tells him: "That's right. I never knew he existed – well, obviously I knew I had a father – but I was raised to think of him as just a sperm donor."

At their startled expressions she adds: "My mother's phrase whenever I asked about him. She was always pretty blunt."

Audrey gravely states: "We heard your mother recently passed away and you have our sympathies. It must be really hard for you."

Amelia hears the true concern in the girl's voice and her words. She says *thank you* and before the silence gets awkward explains: "The shock of meeting Chris, my father, has kinda pushed other thoughts out of my mind. I mean, here's this guy who I know nothing about but who is legally responsible for me and he's a complete stranger. Isn't that crazy? He even has a different name than me, my last name is Coppley. It's really weird, you know?"

"But he's a nice guy, right? I've seen him around and he's hot for somebody his age," says Joanna. Andy elbows her shaking his head but Joanna doesn't stop. "What? he is! So he lets you call him Chris?"

"I never asked for permission, I mean what am I supposed to call him? *Father* sounds stupid and *Dad* doesn't feel right."

"Maybe it will, later on, like," puts in Esther. She didn't expect everyone to be so interested in Amelia and doesn't like being sidelined from their conversation.

The teenagers of Sweet Berry Cove don't date each other, they go out in groups continuing the friendships they formed as toddlers. Anyone new attracts all kinds of interest, particularly when it's another teen.

Somewhat shortly she adds: "Anyhow, eat your cone it's starting to drip."

Amelia is grateful for the break from the quizzing but knows there will be many more questions from these people and others. She licks up the running drips of ice-cream so quickly brain freeze threatens. Slowing down she concentrates on eating her snack while listening to the talk around her.

Esther quickly scans the customers in the shop before asking: "Where's John? He knows we all planned to meet up on our first day of Christmas vacation so I expected him to be here by now."

"He's coming. He had to go and get some new guy called Simon. This guy is Jacky Paulson's grandson and he's staying here for the whole school break."

"Ugh, poor guy! old Paulson is such a grump," comments Andy.

Joanna agrees: "I know! he bashes into you with that walker of his and never even says *sorry*. And if this Simon is anything like his grandfather I don't wanna hang out with him."

Blaine complains: "Huh! we don't have a choice, you know what our parents are like *be nice, be polite, make the newbie feel welcome*."

He looks up and catching Amelia's eye suddenly looks embarrassed. "I don't mean you," he says loudly, adding in a mumble: "You seem really nice."

Audrey rolls her eyes and says: "Give the guy a chance, I mean can you imagine having to stay at Mr. Paulson's place? Why is he doing that, do you know?"

"I heard his parents are off to Europe on a second honeymoon."

"Oh eww!" From the varying looks of disgust on their faces all the teens share Esther's reaction.

Before anyone can comment a blast of cold air swirls through the room. Two teenage boys come in, quickly pushing the door shut behind them. John is average-looking in build, height, and coloring, but the youth with him has the face of a movie star. He's quite tall with dark hair that flops down over bright blue eyes and a wide white grin. The four girls all sit straighter and study the new arrival with interest.

The boys get their order and come to join the group. The eight teenagers are soon engaged in several conversations with their phones out texting and sharing memes and music videos. Loud laughter, sham *eww, so gross!* indignation, and giggles fill the air.

As is common among their age group there's constant fidgeting movement: twirling long hair, shoulders swaying and toes tapping to the beat, a vibrating leg, knuckles cracking, and sitting sideways with their limbs all folded up.

The dull afternoon sun is setting when a woman comes in and greets Sandy Sunday with the promise *I'll get these kids out of your hair now.*

"Come on, I've got the station wagon and can squeeze you all in. No point dragging anyone else's parents out in this weather."

"Hey thanks, Mom," says Audrey. She points to the new faces introducing them: "This is Amelia, Helena's step-daughter, and he's Simon, Jacky Paulson's grandson."

"Well, well one of you I've heard plenty about and absolutely nothing about the other. Isn't that the way of things? Come along, then."

Audrey sits up front beside her mother while Esther, Amelia, and Simon take the first row. The girls glare daggers at Joanna who climbs onto Simon's lap saying *I can just squeeze in here.*

Blaine, John, and Andy share the back-seat along with bags of shopping. Mrs. Ardrossan speaks non-stop during the drive talking about the unusually cold weather, the crowded stores in SLO, and the upcoming Christmas Party sponsored by the Sweet Berry Cove Farmers Cooperative.

Joanna gets dropped off first and both Andy and Blaine say they'll get out too. Andy's family are farmers but he's staying in the village tonight and Blaine's place is just up the block.

Next stop unloads John and Simon. When the car starts up again Audrey swivels round to exchange a knowing look with the two remaining girls saying: "I saw it all from the side-mirror," just as Esther exclaimed: "She's unbelievable!"

"Are you girls talking about Joanna Berridge? You don't need to worry about her sitting on Simon's knee, that boy only had eyes for Amelia."

Esther's slight frown at that remark turns into a scowl when she sees Amelia's happy smile. Audrey turns back in her seat and meeting her mother's eye shares a secret smirk.

In a small town every little drama counts which prods Mrs. Ardrossan to ask: "By the way, did Sandy Sunday have an update on Miz Tally? I ran into that Janice Peart who had a worrying story to tell."

News Shared

Milly doesn't know the make of Chris Larch's car but she can tell the luxury sedan is an expensive model. The vehicle has pulled into the kitchen yard and she can see by their silhouettes that two people are inside. She assumes the passenger is Helena. They sit outside for a whole minute and just when Milly moves to the kitchen door both car doors open and the Larches step out.

Milly waves at them to *hurry in out of the cold* and moments later the guests are seated at the kitchen table while Milly goes to see who else is at home.

Returning with the news that all three of the Young men are here and will be joining them shortly Milly excuses herself to go back to stirring a lamb stew on the stove.

"It smells delicious—" begins Helena just as Milly invites them to stay for supper.

"Oh I wasn't angling for a meal," Helena exclaims. "We're just here to pick up Amelia before getting Mom and going into SLO. We've got reservations for dinner at Antonacci's, Mom's favorite restaurant."

"Antonacci's?" repeats Samuel as he comes into the room. "Oh you're in for a treat! the food there is excellent."

Amos and Daniel arrive in the kitchen and hearing his father's comment Amos agrees. "It's pricey but totally worth every nickel. The serving portions are huge, too."

"And you know that must be true if my son is satisfied," jokes Samuel.

Bernie has accompanied the brothers in and now heads straight for Chris angling his head for another good ear-scratching.

"Martha got a flyer advertising their Table d'Hote menu. All week it features *traditional Italian Christmas dishes* and the place is being decorated for the holidays so it's all very festive and we're looking forward to that."

Daniel comments that he's never been to Antonacci's and both Amos and Samuel insist he take Milly there before the special holiday menu is over.

All eyes turn her way and she smiles widely enough to show her dimples as she teases: "Then who is going to feed you folks?"

"Not me!" declares Nora, coming into the kitchen just in time to hear the question. "These ingrates won't eat my cooking now that you've spoiled them rotten, Milly. We'll just have to get take-out if you're not here."

"Or we could join them? Make a double-date out of it."

Amos is enthusiastic but seeing a flash of disappointment in Milly's eyes Nora says: "We'll have to take a rain-check until the new year, hon, our social calendar is full. But you two must let us know all about it."

They all hear a car pull into the yard and looking out the window over the sink Milly sees Esther stepping out.

"The girls are back home now," she says.

"Did they really did go for an ice-cream? Today?" Chris is incredulous making Samuel chuckle at the look on the younger man's face.

"It's a steep learning curve to understand anything teenagers do, Chris. Unfortunately you're being thrown in at the deep end of the pool."

Slipping her hand into the crook of her husband's elbow Helena says: "Don't worry hon, we'll sink or swim together."

Daniel has worked his way around the table to stand beside Milly. Leaning in he murmurs *just like you and me will be learning how to train Bernie, our very own bundle of joy.* Milly swallows air while struggling not to laugh which makes her burp, much to Daniel's delight.

She fakes a cough to cover up but it isn't necessary. The girls have come inside and Bernie is headbutting them for pats and barking for attention.

Helena and Chris are ready to get going once Amelia comes in. Samuel tells her to *keep the warm gear you borrowed because you'll need it over the next few days.*

"Helena, there's an idea for a Christmas present!" Nora exclaims.

The Larches say goodnight and the family head into the dining-room to have their supper. Daniel helps Milly by carrying the large tureen of stew while she follows with warm bread.

"This smells so good, Milly," Amos is always appreciative of her cooking. "That's different looking bread, what kind is it?"

"I made soda bread for a change. It's got a distinctive flavor because it uses baking soda and butttermilk. And being Irish it goes well with Irish Stew."

Daniel ladled out the thick broth full with vegetables and chunks of tender lamb into bowls for everyone. Soon they're all eating and complimenting the meal.

"This bread is delicious, too."

"It's really easy to make—"

Interrupting Amos says: "Now Milly, don't tease Nora. We all know nothing is easy when she's in the kitchen..."

"Huh!" his wife says warning him: "I haven't bought your Christmas present yet so keep it up and you'll be getting a lump of coal."

Before he can answer Nora turns to Milly saying: "This really is an excellent meal, so tasty! We're very lucky to have you, Milly."

"Hear, hear!" chants Samuel and they all raise their respective glasses of cider or fruit juice in a toast to the cook.

After their dinner things have been cleared away and the kitchen tidied the family move into the sitting-room around the fire.

"Oh it smells lovely, this is that apple wood Hannah was telling me about, isn't it?"

"That's right, Milly. You can tell the difference between this and the usual firewood, huh?"

"Oh you can't miss it."

"And the aroma fills up the whole place, making it welcoming and cosy."

"So Esther, tell us all the news from The Cove."

The girl is sitting cross-legged on the floor, staring into the fire, but now she turns to face her father with an update on their neighbors.

"Well, everyone wanted to know all about Amelia but nobody was rude to her or anything like that. 'Course it's good that Janice Peart wasn't around poking her nose in because that one has no idea about boundaries."

Nora and Milly exchange a glance at hearing this favorite phrase of Hannah's repeated.

"And it turns out mean old Jacky Paulson has a grandson called Simon. He showed up with John and he's the whole meal, like totally fire."

Hesitantly Samuel says: "Which is a good thing?"

"Just ask Joanna! She threw herself at him but he wasn't interested in her. Now that Amelia's here Joanna has got some competition."

Esther turns back to the fire and the adults discuss the homes they'll be building shortly. The bulk of the construction has to be done before the rush of Spring farm work takes up everyone's time.

Daniel is sitting close to Milly and slips his arm around her shoulders. He lifts a strand of her hair and curls it round his finger. Tugging gently he draws her attention and the two exchange contented looks.

Daniel is being unusually touchy-feely tonight, she thinks with a pleased smile.

"Oh I forgot about Miz Tally," Esther announces. The elderly woman is one of their closest friends and they all want to hear any news of her.

"I didn't hear it at Sunday's but on the drive home Mrs. Adrossan asked if there was an update on Miz Tally's condition because that Janice Peart was worrying about her health."

"Oh no!" cries Milly in dismay.

Daniel tightens his embrace reminding her that "That Janice Peart exaggerates to make herself look important. Miz Tally probably just has a head cold."

"Oh I hope you're right, Daniel," she says, her brow creased with worry.

"You know son, at her age the least little thing can become serious," puts in Samuel.

"True, but no matter what we all say and think of that Janice Peart she is a very good friend and neighbor to Miz Tally and she'll keep an eye on her."

Nora wryly adds: "And she'll share frequent bulletins, too!"

Daniel is Dismissive

At breakfast Milly asks Daniel if the two of them can go shopping to buy her car but he tells her she doesn't need one.

"You can always borrow any of the farm vehicles, any time."

Surprised, she answers: "No, I'd like to have a car of my own."

"Of your own? Why? What difference does it make?" He just shakes his head at her statement.

"Well... because I want one and I can afford it," she answers sharply.

"Oh right, you and your money. Sometimes it feels like there's a wheelbarrow full of cash standing here creating a barrier between us, Milly."

In the shocked silence that follows he immediately regrets his harsh words seeing the stricken expression on Milly's face.

Before he can apologize Nora speaks up saying: "I'm going into SLO today, Milly. I need to finish my Christmas shopping, but come with me and we'll stop at a dealership while we're there if you like."

Nora's been off work since Monday when the elementary school closed for the holidays.

Carefully avoiding Daniel's eye Milly enthuses: "That would be great! thanks, Nora. When are you going to go? I've got the Farm Shop to open–"

"I'll take over the shop for today, Milly," offers Samuel. She smiles at him gratefully.

Nora nods her thanks to Samuel saying: "Perfect! We'll go right after breakfast, if that works for you?"

Hannah has come in and overhearing their conversation tells Milly, "I'm here now to take care of the breakfast things so you go ahead. It's best to get there early if you want to avoid the holiday crowds."

"Thank you, Hannah. I'll just go grab my purse, Nora," Milly says as she leaves.

"I'll meet you at the front door. Do you think we'll need boots, Amos?"

Looking out the window her husband answers: "It was pretty overcast first thing but now those clouds have blown over so I think you'll be okay but wear the fancy shoes that have got good traction in case it gets slippery."

Leaning over to give him a kiss Nora comments: "You do like to fuss, don't you?"

Amos gives her a wink and a smirk, asking: "Do you need any money?"

"No, I'm good thanks. Does anyone need anything while we're there?"

The men all shake their heads *no* so with a wave Nora heads out. Listening until he hears the front door close Samuel turns to Daniel with a sigh.

"What don't you understand about Milly wanting her own car? You got yourself that old pickup within a week of turning sixteen. I remember how excited you were, you couldn't wait *to have your own wheels* as you put it."

"Yeah, but as you said I was sixteen, Dad. Milly's not a kid."

"No she isn't, but she's been denied a lot of things, material things and more - like not getting to grow up as a normal kid - so let her enjoy getting a car of her own now that she can."

"Well... when you put it that way... but you know it isn't necessary–" begins Daniel.

Samuel interrupts him saying, "Son, think about it from her point of view. We take the freedom of mobility for granted but we all have our own vehicles. If anyone took that away from us we'd sure feel it."

"Okay, I get what you're saying but there's no need for her to waste her money."

Shaking his head Samuel begs his son to *use your imagination!* When Daniel frowns, not understanding, Samuel spells it out. "Maybe – just maybe – Milly *wants* to waste some of it. She's finally got money of her own and she wants to spend it. Let her enjoy this moment by enjoying it with her."

Daniel's face holds a stubborn expression but Samuel knows his younger son is slow to come to decisions and very much the type to mull things over and over first. He has faith Daniel will figure it out.

Amos can't resist the opportunity to be the provocative big brother: "You know Daniel, you're pretty bossy for a man who hasn't *put a ring on it* yet."

Samuel barks out a laugh in surprise but then turns towards his youngest son with a hopeful expression.

"As a matter of fact I'm giving Milly a ring for Christmas," Daniel retorts.

"Oh bro, as her Christmas present?" Amos shakes his head.

He's still teasing Daniel but truthfully says: "I don't recommend that at all. For one thing it makes you look cheap, and for another – do you really want to propose on Christmas morning with all of us hearing every word while we're sitting around in our pajamas?"

Daniel frowns over Amos's words and thinks for a moment before replying: "So New Year's Eve would be a better time to propose?"

Amos just gives his brother an exasperated look before turning to Samuel and shrugging his shoulders.

Samuel's tone is gentle when he tells Daniel: "Son, it doesn't have to be a special occasion, it's the proposal itself that makes the day special. It doesn't matter what the date is."

Amos chimes in to add: "Milly is probably expecting a ring for Christmas and if you wait til New Year's she'll be miserable from disappointment all week, so figure it out!"

"But you just said Christmas isn't a good time—"

"That's right! You need to surprise her before Christmas."

"And if you truly are planning to get engaged to Milly I'll be the first to congratulate you on a wonderful choice, Daniel."

Milly and Nora Go Shopping

The air is chilly but both Milly and Nora are thankful they're not too heavily bundled as they walk in and out of the overheated stores. The sidewalks are bustling with the Christmas-shopping crowds. Business is brisk for the street vendors selling roasted chestnuts and steaming hot chocolate drinks.

"It's so festive and full of Christmas spirit!" exclaims Milly taking in all the decorations hanging from the street lights and the miniature fir trees lit up in the store windows. Holiday music piped from speakers competes with carolers singing and shaking tambourines while collecting for charity.

It's early enough in the day that the mood is light. Shoppers are filled with anticipation instead of frustration, and the store clerks aren't yet frazzled by demanding customers and non-stop activity.

The two women have a successful couple of hours finding gifts and crossing names off their lists. "Do you want to stop for a coffee and a muffin? or go straight to the car dealership?" Nora asks Milly.

"I noticed the cafés are all awfully busy so if it's all the same to you Nora, I'd rather skip the coffee and go see what's available for a car. I gave it a lot of thought and decided I want to get a brand-new car."

"Good for you!" Nora says with approval. "I don't know anything about cars so I bought mine new and it's never given me any trouble. Of course I keep it properly serviced although nowadays Amos does the oil changes for me."

In the parking lot they load their purchases into the trunk of the car. Milly murmurs *uh-oh* and nudges Nora's who now sees that there are two cars vying to claim her parking space.

"Well, I feel sorry for the red car because the way I'm parked means I can only go one way and when I pull out that black car will be able to grab the spot first."

"Christmas goodwill gets stretched thin!" Milly stage-whispers, biting her lip to hide her smile.

Carefully navigating away from the hovering cars Nora gets them on the road to the car dealership located on the outskirts of town, on the way back to Sweet Berry Cove.

Even in daytime they can see the strings of red and green lights flicker over the cars in the lot The windows of the showroom are decorated with paintings of cartoon characters engaging in winter sports, and inside there's an enormous white Christmas tree done up with silver and gold ornaments.

Milly pauses to look at some cars but Nora leads her away saying: "No, these are the used, oh excuse me, the *pre-owned* vehicles. The new ones are inside."

Two attractive customers soon have the attention of all the salesmen on the floor. The flattery and light-hearted banter has Milly blushing and Nora twiddling her fingers to show off her wedding ring but it's all in fun and they're having a good time.

Over the next hour they learn about various features and financing plans and delivery schedules. Milly falls in love with a sporty two-seater. She finds the price shocking but before she can say *no, that's way too expensive* Nora is dickering with the man. He's making extravagant gestures of how she's killing him but since it's Christmas... Milly tells him she'll be paying cash and he puts together an appealing offer.

Back at the farmhouse both women are bubbling over with excitement and their enthusiasm is contagious. Daniel sees how Milly's eyes sparkle and recalling what his father said he uncomfortably experiences a twinge of shame over his earlier attitude.

Nora is teasing Amos about all the flirting that went on and ends up giggling at his fake growl. "So let's go see this wonderful new car," he states.

"Oh I didn't buy it yet. I couldn't do that without Daniel seeing it first." Milly turns to him hopefully and he smiles saying: "We'll go tomorrow morning, okay?"

Throwing her arms around his neck she happily answers: "Definitely okay."

Over her shoulder Daniel sees his father nod in approval.

Sitting at the kitchen table they hear Esther complain *not again!* Samuel asks his daughter *what's wrong?*

She explains: "I wanted to see Amelia but she's made plans to go out with Simon. Again. They're going to the show and it's a movie I wanted to see, too," she finishes with a pout.

"Well just call up one of your other girlfriends, Audrey or Joanne, and go with them," Simon states, not understanding his daughter's real grievance. Milly has an idea what the actual problem is, but she thinks to herself *if Nora's not saying anything I won't either.*

Miz Tally Rushed to Hospital

Spending the day in San Luis Obispo meant the two women missed the drama of an ambulance, siren blaring, arriving in Sweet Berry Cove to rush Miz Tally to the hospital. They soon heard all about it, and their dinner kept getting interrupted by phone-calls.

Hannah is the first to pass on the news but she doesn't have a lot to relate.

"I was told by Dorothy—" turning to Milly she explains "She's Doc Watkins nurse so this isn't hearsay, it's factual and true. Anyhow she said that Miz Tally fell ill and the Doctor was called in and he ordered an ambulance to take her to the hospital.

Now Dorothy emphasized that she doesn't actually *know anything* and is only guessing, but said Doc Watkins has been concerned about Miz Tally for some time because she's awfully old to be living on her own. At that age dehydration is an issue, resistance to germs is low, and of course bones are brittle and easily broken.

So she said it's entirely possible – even likely – that the trip might just be precautionary."

"Let's hope it is a case of the good doctor choosing to *err on the side of caution*," says Samuel. "I realize she's extremely old but I've known Tallulah all my life and she's a tough old gal."

"I hope you're right, but to rush her all the way to the hospital in SLO—"

Interrupting Milly Hannah says: "Oh she's not in SLO. No, no, she's at our local care home."

"Sweet Berry Cove Rest Home, and that's not far," answers Nora.

Amos explains that it's a not-for-profit facility funded by the Sweet Berry Cove Farmers' Cooperative. Since the closest hospital isn't close at all The Cove's non-surgical cases get sent to the rest home for treatment and recuperation.

"It's small and locally staffed so patients are among familiar faces, and are far less likely to come down with those horrible infections people seem to pick up in big hospitals," Nora adds.

"Well that's good news, right? I mean as good as can be in a situation like this," Milly trails off uncertainly.

From the first time they met, months ago, Milly has felt an affinity with Miz Tally. She'd originally thought it was just because the woman was elderly and Milly had grown up surrounded by seniors. But they both developed a real liking for each other and now Milly can't help but worry about her friend.

Seeing her distress Samuel lays his work-roughened hand on top of her much smaller one and gently squeezes while assuring her that *all will be well.*

Confrontation

"Oh no, oh that's awful. The dreadful news about Miz Tally being rushed to hospital is bad enough, but now there's this nasty story being spread around?" Nora is at the local Library having dropped in this morning to return a book.

The library is part of the school and Verna, or maybe it's Myrna? Harrigan passes on the gossip. "Pure tittle-tattle I'm sure, and not something I would normally repeat, but in this case I think it's best for the Young's to know what's being said."

"Yes, of course. Thank you for sharing that with me. But oh, what am I going to say to the family? To say nothing of poor Milly. No doubt there are still some townspeople believing she stole the Farm Shop money from the safe when Amos and I had it all along. But people will believe what they like and the very worst interpretation seems to be what they like best."

Nodding sagely Miss Harrigan, Myrna as it happens, continues: "That Janice Peart said it certainly wasn't the chicken broth she got from the shop. That was on Monday. She bought it for Miz Tally when she was first feeling poorly. Oh Verna! that means the poor soul was already ill four days ago. Janice said she'd had some of the broth herself and she's fine. No, she's blaming something else but of course she can't say what because she doesn't know."

"Yet that doesn't stop her tongue from wagging. Oh that woman!" Nora says in exasperation. "To think that she's spreading rumors about Miz Tally getting food poisoning from the Farm Shop. From something that Milly cooked or baked. It's just too awful!"

Nora soon discovers that everyone she meets that morning is passing on the story with speculation and embellishments. Preoccupied with her frustrated thoughts she collides with Stephen Smithson in the doorway of the General Store. He apologizes but she rightfully takes the blame for not watching her step.

"I'm so sorry, Reverend. I'm distracted. I heard something disturbing and the story keeps snowballing into a nasty, sordid tale."

Taking her by the arm Reverend Smithson steers Nora out of the way of foot traffic leading the two of them to one of the many benches the village merchants provide for shoppers to rest.

"I suspect it's the same vile rumor I just heard in the Post Office. Jay Somers served me, of course, but as soon as he started talking Kay jumped right in to add her poisonous two-cent's worth. Oh, I shouldn't say that, but honestly I just saw red. I spoke quite harshly to both of them and I'm not in the least bit sorry about it.

I not only reprimanded them for spreading stories but I reminded them of their responsibility to maintain good relations with everyone in the village."

"So you heard about Miz Tally taking ill and Milly's baking being blamed?"

"I knew about Tallulah yesterday, I saw the ambulance and gave Doc Watkins a call. But I just heard this horrible rumor now and insisted on knowing where this came from.

It was busy in the store and I asked for *anyone who knew anything to speak up*. A few more customers joined in the conversation and after much delaying and plenty of *I don't remember, don't quote* me, and *I'm not positive* comments I traced it back to that Janice Peart.

I told the Somers I wished they were as hesitant to pass on gossip as they were to reveal the source. Then I demanded *what proof did Janice*

Peart provide? and all I got were embarrassed mumbles. It makes me so angry. Margaret, my housekeeper, better not be involved in it this time."

Exasperated Nora cried: "What on earth does that Janice Peart have against Milly?"

"Probably nothing more than she's a pretty and popular young woman so stories about her quickly gain traction."

Bitterly Nora retorts: "Hasn't she been victimized enough by falsehoods? You handled that business with Esther very well Reverend, and I thought it was all was *done and dusted*. Now this. I dread telling Milly but I know have to."

She sighs so deeply Stephen offers to provide moral support. He accompanies Nora back to the farmhouse. During the short walk they discuss different ways to approach the subject. Nora decides she should speak to Milly privately first so she sends the Reverend to go find his friend Samuel.

Arriving in the kitchen Nora starts off by saying that she regrets being *the bearer of bad news* but must inform Milly of something that's being gossiped about in The Cove. She ends up apologetically relaying the news.

Milly, usually so even-tempered, instantly flares up. It was one thing when folks thought she'd stolen money from her employer which bothered her, but she knew she hadn't done anything wrong. She was confident that the truth would come out eventually and it did. But to have unfounded and false accusations about the safety of her food was infuriating.

"What am I supposed to have poisoned my friend with?" she demands.

"Nobody knows, they're all just repeating what the Janice Peart said about it having come from the Farm Shop. Milly, I know that's not true, but let's play *Devil's Advocate* for a moment and try to figure out if there is any product that's even remotely possible to blame? Like something with cream or whipped cream?"

Nora's attempted diplomacy fails as Milly practically shouts "I am *ruthless* when it comes discarding anything past its date—"

The men hear raised voices coming from the kitchen and hurry in to find out what's going on. Milly is magnificent in her anger. She's livid, claiming herself *ready to challenge anyone who impugns the food I prepare.*

"That Janice Peart—" begins Samuel but Milly interrupts him.

"I'll clear my name and yours, Samuel. I'll demand the old gossip show her proof and since she can't I'll tell her to keep her uncharitable thoughts to herself! After she publicly apologizes."

Daniel is surprised to see Milly in this fiery mood with determination flashing in her eyes. She's revealing hidden strengths that intrigue him, making him wonder what else he can discover about his normally demure and self-contained fiancée.

"We'll fight this together, sweetheart," he says trying to mollify his little spitfire.

The part of Milly's mind that isn't taken up with exacting justice melts slightly at the endearment. "Oh I'm sorry Daniel, but getting my car will have to wait, I want to see Miz Tally as soon as possible. Can you look after the Farm Shop again today Samuel? I'm sorry to impose but—"

"It's no imposition, Milly. Yesterday was pretty quiet and I was wishing I'd brought my book but the way the gossip mill is churning I expect I'll have plenty of curious folks coming in today."

Bitterly Milly says: "But probably not to buy, they'll be too worried about getting poisoned."

"Oh my dear, I'm sure we'll get the real story soon and in the meantime I'll make the nosy ones so uncomfortable they'll have to buy something even if they throw it out once they're back home."

"But that's just..." Milly breaks off and gives Samuel a devilish smirk before ending her sentence: "Good!" to surprised laughter.

Daniel drives the two of them in his old truck. It's a short ride to the rest home. They park in the graveled lot of a one-story brick building and Milly, who visited the hospital in SLO when Daniel was there, looks at this small facility with interest. It's utilitarian in style, but she can see rose bushes currently wrapped up for winter, which must make it look pretty.

Opening the door into the homey building Daniel ushers Milly inside. Looking around she's impressed by the comfortable atmosphere with its clean but not antiseptic smell.

Before they can even ask the woman at the front desk about Miz Tally Janice Peart's voice shrilly declaims: "You've got some nerve showing your face here!"

What had been an empty reception area is suddenly populated with a variety of people, some in medical clothing, some visitors, and all with curious faces. Refusing to back down Milly steps towards her accuser demanding to know *what, exactly, do you mean by that?*

Janice sputters that *everyone knows* but Milly interrupts loudly insisting: "Janice, produce your proof."

Before she can reply Milly continues: "Miz Tally's doctors are here so let's ask them, shall we? Because Janice Peart you have spread a totally unfounded accusation that could have a devastating effect on the Young's Family Farm Shop. This is very serious and I will charge you with slander if I find you've acted with malicious intent."

The older woman's face blanches but she rallies defending herself by stating: "Miz Tally was getting all her food from your place so it stands to reason that's what made her sick."

"That's it? That's the basis of your scurrilous attack on the integrity of my products? Miz Tally is loved by everyone and she's frequently gifted food treats by her friends, neighbors, and all those nieces and nephews she has. How dare you, madame!" she ends in a hiss.

In the silence that follows Milly's rebuke it almost seems like the audience will break into spontaneous applause. A wave of satisfaction wafts from the crowd to see Janice Peart get her comeuppance. Many residents of the Cove have suffered from her snide innuendos and barbed insults so word will travel quickly about this confrontation with Milly Clarke.

Daniel feels Milly's body vibrating with emotion as he draws her close, throwing a protective arm across her shoulders. He's deeply impressed with her fighting spirit and thankful he didn't ruin things between them over her wanting to buy a car.

When he asks the receptionist *is Miz Tally seeing visitors?* that breaks the spell and people drift back to what they were doing before the outburst.

Miz Tally is awake and lying in the hospital bed. She's dressed in a pretty and feminine bed jacket but its delicate rose shade can't give her any color, her face is as pale as the pillowcase she's resting on. A very long braid of white hair is laid down her body. She looks impossibly small tucked into the bedding and Milly's heart wrenches at the sight.

Before she can voice her concern Miz Tally softly speaks assuring the young couple that she's responding well to the doctor's treatment and feeling much better than she was. "I heard your set-to with Janice just now–"

Milly interrupts saying she's so sorry for disturbing the patient but Miz Tally simply lifts a thin hand to stop the apology insisting: "It perked me right up! I wish I could have seen Janice's face. Now I'm being unkind considering I owe her so much. Did you know she's the one who insisted the doctor send an ambulance to fetch me here?

But she has no right to make accusations because none of us know what I ate that caused this runny tummy."

Daniel interjects: "Miz Tally! A bout of gastroenteritis is hardly just an upset stomach. It's exhausting, painful and dehydrating which leads to serious illness."

Although her smile is weak it's full of Miz Tally's trademark merriment. Suddenly both Milly and Daniel feel their shoulders slump in relief. Samuel was right: Miz Tally is a fighter and she is going to be okay.

Esther is Jealous

Peter Showalty enjoys a daily walk along the beach. The round trip up and down the bluffs gives him the healthy workout that he needs after sitting behind his desk for hours. Not that he sits all day. He's often seen patrolling the hallways ready to hustle loitering students back to their classrooms, or helping to referee a game in the gym.

He gets his to-go mug filled with coffee at Sunday's Ice Cream Shoppe and on days like today he's especially grateful for the hot drink. He always begins walking against the wind so he can enjoy the push at his back on his return trip.

Today it's especially strong and his ears are suffering in the biting cold. That's why he's so surprised to see someone huddled in a wind-break under a ridge of sea grasses. He veers towards the figure, it's a woman, to check everything is okay. Coming close he realizes it's a girl, it's Esther Young. She's sitting hunched up with her arms wrapped around her legs and her face looking pinched and miserable.

"Esther, what's happened? What's wrong?"

She looks up and her expression is so unhappy. Her eyes are still full of tears, and her reddened nose shows she's been crying for awhile.

"Oh Principal Showalty I'm upset because... because it's unfair that Amelia just got here and already she and Simon Paulson are a couple and I liked him too!"

"You're talking about Jacky Paulson's grandson? Is that who this Simon is?"

"Yes, and we both met him at the same time and, well, we were um... teasing each other about him, and saying we both liked him and I guess we were sorta competing for him."

"Like a game? It was a bet or no, not that, more like a challenge between you and Amelia?"

"Yeah well... sort of, I mean we didn't actually say it out loud or anything but we both knew."

"Ahhh, and you say the boy chose Amelia?"

"Uh-huh but you know she like must have let him do stuff, um like, you know, like touching her or something—"

Peter is quite firm when he interrupts Esther to explain just how damaging rumors and speculation can be to someone's reputation. How gossip can cause real hurt and harm.

Without actually mentioning it they both remember how many of the villagers ostracized Milly when they suspected she stole money from the Farm Shop safe. Esther played a role in that mix-up.

Under Peter's intense scrutiny she now admits that she doesn't *really* think anything actually happened between Simon and Amelia, she's just feeling sorry for herself.

"I know I have a problem with jealousy, but the truth is I mind losing Amelia's company more than I care about being Simon's girlfriend."

Peter nods in understanding then he talks about his feelings for Milly Clarke and how he had to step aside when it became obvious that she and Daniel had feelings for each other.

"It's a very small community here Esther, and we all have to get along. It's vital not to spread rumors or do anything that will cause people to gossip about you. Most of your contemporaries will end up settling down here so Sweet Berry Cove will probably be your home for a long time. Even if it isn't, if, for example, you move away for your career or marriage, you'll definitely return from time to time. You'll want to be sure your memories are happy ones, and that people think well of you."

Sighing the girl replies: "I know you're right, Principal Showalty. I remember how Daniel just hated everybody knowing his business when Helena left him to marry Christopher Larch."

"That's a very good example. People spoke about your brother becoming gloomy and grouchy and everyone had an opinion on whether the break-up was a good or bad thing.

You know, I hear an awful lot of what goes on from the conversations between my secretary, Mrs. Robson, and the Miss Harrigan's from the Library," he pauses to chuckle before adding: "They were just reeling after hearing the story behind the Larches separation. It really is an unbelievable story yet Amelia exists so it must be true.

The women gossiped, speculated, and opined then righteously claimed that *we aren't telling tales, only sharing the news.*"

"Oh for sure, they always know what's happening and they pass it on to everyone, too."

"Now from what I understand the Paulson boy is only here for the Christmas vacation, is that right?"

"Yeah, he goes back home to San Diego when school starts in January."

"Well, San Diego is quite a long ways away, especially for teenagers who can't freely travel around. I think you'll have your friend back again before you know it."

"She really is my friend you know, we hit it off right away, and I guess it's only natural that she's gonna get a lot of attention because of her parents and everything."

Esther's face takes on a more mature look as her gaze drifts out across the bay, the darker waters of the Pacific stretching out as far as the eye can see.

Peter Showalty once again marvels to himself over the miracle of watching children grow to become adults. Esther has a long way to go yet but she's already experiencing the complexity of friendships. Discovering the joy of emotional involvement and the added dimension it brings to life.

Quietly she asks: "I'm being silly, aren't I?"

"You're being human, and you're going to be all right."

Encouraged by her grateful smile he drops his voice saying: "Now I'm going to be a gossip and ask if it's true that Milly gave Janice Peart a tongue-lashing at the Nursing Home?"

Laughing, Esther confirms that Milly most definitely did. "When Nora brought the news home from the village that morning Milly was furious! Amos said with all the yelling he thought Milly and Nora were fighting which he couldn't imagine at all, but it was just Milly venting. She really went into a rage and I guess she doubled-down on it when she actually saw that Janice Peart."

Peter joins in the laughter exclaiming: "Oh I wish I'd been there! These quiet types are shockingly magnificent when they finally explode!"

There's a tinge of regret in his voice but Esther doesn't notice. She stands up exclaiming at the cold as if she's suddenly just noticed it.

"C'mon then," Peter says straightening up, "a brisk walk will soon warm us up."

"Walk? No way, I'm running!" declares Esther with a *whoop* and runs off with the energy of youth.

So yet another story about Milly Clarke was making the rounds in The Cove. The majority applauded her actions knowing full well that Janice Peart was a gossip-monger who wouldn't let facts get in her way. Most felt it was high time the older woman was taken down a peg or two.

Still, there were those who repeated the old saw about *no smoke without fire*. These people happily dredged up the theft rumor, conveniently brushing off the explanation by saying *I always thought there was more to that story that never came out* and nodding wisely at each other.

Daniel's Surprise

Milly decides a drink of herbal tea will relax her enough to sleep. *It's been an eventful day*, she thinks ruefully, *but I don't regret either of my outbursts. I am 100 percent confident in the food I prepare.*

Being in the tidy kitchen, only lit by the light over the stove, calms her. *This is my wheelhouse. This is where I create my products and where I feed the family. It's a practical place and I'm a practical woman. Running a family farm is a business and I have my place in it.*

Romantic dreams are just that – dreams. I'll live a life of want and disappointment if I go chasing after a fantasy.

These thoughts have been playing through her mind all evening and now she feels settled. *Acceptance is good, and if I just keep telling myself that then eventually I'm sure I will come to accept and appreciate what I have. That's the key, really. Appreciation, gratitude, and acceptance are the means to achieve serenity.*

Before she plugs in the kettle Daniel enters the kitchen. Taking hold of Milly's hand he leads her out of the room through the front hall and outside to the porch.

It's sheltered out here because every December they put up wooden shutters to protect from the cold winds. Sometimes in the summer one or two people, usually young visitors like their twin cousins, will sleep on the porch in sleeping bags. These same sleeping bags make a warm, comfy seat on the rocker-swing in the winter.

A pile of old quilts and blankets is stacked just inside the front door and Daniel scoops up a couple with his free hand on the way out. Sitting down he settles Milly in his lap, pinning her in place with one arm.

"Daniel! what are you doing–" she begins, feeling flustered, but he lays a thick finger against her lips for silence.

"I want to have a good look at you, Milly, and I'm going to tell you what I see. I suspect that might not tally with what you think I see… so here goes."

His eyes move up to the crown of her head and with his free hand he runs his fingers through her long locks.

Teasing out a few strands he says: "These red highlights… no, not red-red what's this color called?"

"Auburn," answers Milly, her voice little more than a whisper.

"That's it, yes. Auburn highlights in your dark brown – brunette – hair that always smells like lavender." He smooths the hair back from her face adding: "I'm sure I've told you before not to let it hang down and hide your pretty face."

Milly is too busy controlling her breathing to reply. She can feel the blush she hates rising. Daniel feels differently about her flushed cheeks, stroking the back of his finger against her heated skin.

"So beautiful when this rosy color floods your face. And your skin is so soft. Give me a smile so I can see your dimples."

Milly looks down, shaking her head and hiding her huge smile. Daniel tips up her chin and she's forced to meet his eyes. She finds such a loving look in those peat-brown depths that butterflies flutter deep inside her. They're flying about filling her with wonder and happiness and smiles.

"There they are!" he exclaims triumphantly. "I can't resist pinching your cheek," and he does so gently. "No, no don't turn your eyes away. I want to see what color they are today."

Laughing lightly Milly chides him saying: "Today? did you forget my eye color? You know they're always blue–"

"Ah but there's blue and there's blue. When you're sitting calm and quiet, reading or writing something, your eyes are almost gray and when you're feeling something strongly they're practically navy. But most of the time they're a nice bright blue."

"They change depending on what color of top I have on. With brown hair and blue eyes I mostly wear pink or blue, that's all it is."

"No, it isn't. Dad and Amos both have blue eyes but theirs are always a light sky-blue. I have my Mom's brown eyes, and they're a light shade too. Milly your eyes do change but not just because of what you're wearing. The color reflects your moods as well."

Milly can only stare – stupidly – she imagines, at Daniel's compliments. He's never spoken like this before and she's flattered, pleased, and far too entranced to utter her usual disclaimers.

"I see a beautiful girl... no, make that a beautiful young woman, with a heartwarming smile, pretty blush, and sparkling eyes. A lovely face framed by long, thick, wavy hair with highlights."

"Oh Daniel," she manages to choke the words out as he cups her face in his warm hand. Turning her head slightly Milly brushes her lips against his palm exhaling on a tender sigh. Daniel runs his thumb over her mouth when she nips her bottom lip showing even white teeth.

Bending down to kiss her he says: "You're perfect."

Milly reaches up to wrap her arms around Daniel's neck. His kiss tastes like apples and cherries, fresh and sweet. Barely pulling away from her mouth he murmurs *lips like velvet, warm and so soft*. Then he returns to his task of kissing her thoroughly and claiming her mouth possessively.

Milly is cuddled against his chest, caged in by his muscular arms, and feeling protected and secure in his strong embrace. His lips press hard with urgency and when the tip of his tongue probes hers Milly is startled at the sensation, like an electric current is running between them.

With a groan Daniel pushes her back leaving enough space between them so he can look down into her face. His hooded eyes are laser-focused on her kiss-swollen lips. In his deep baritone he quietly states:

"I don't dare study and describe the rest of you, not yet, but know that the size and shape of you fits perfectly perched on my knee and I could happily sit like this for hours."

Milly's eyes really do twinkle full of the dazzling emotion, the love, running through her veins with every beat of her heart. She can't believe how eloquently Daniel *my Daniel!* is complimenting her. He never speaks lightly meaning his words are sincere, and the warmth of his love suffuses her being.

"In case the kiss didn't tell you clearly enough hear me now Milly when I say I love you, I love you, I love you." With each iteration he bestows a kiss on her forehead, her cheek, and the tip of her nose making her chuckle.

"I fought against it, you know. I fought against it so hard," he says, slightly shaking his head.

"The very first time I laid eyes on you, standing in the rain outside the kitchen door with a big suitcase at your feet and your lovely face full of determination, I knew I had to harden my heart to protect it. Remember? You were worn out after your long day of travel, and tearful at my rudeness, and all I wanted was to comfort and cuddle you. I had to turn away before I did something stupid."

Thinking back to that night Milly whispers: "Of course I remember. I thought it was a crying shame to waste such a handsome face on such a bad-tempered man."

"You thought – think - I'm handsome?" he prods her.

She pushes his hand away stating: "You shave in front of a mirror every morning so you know perfectly well what you look like."

He tips his head back and squints down at her with a smirk before continuing: "I never did fall in love with you, you know. No, I didn't fall, I was pushed and conquered. It had nothing to do with me, it was all down to you.

I was so busy keeping a tight rein on my feelings I never noticed how you crept up through my defences and captured my heart. You won. Every breath in my body belongs to you, Milly."

Her lips are parted as if his words are giving her the very air that she's breathing in as deeply as she can.

Daniel's right arm is resting along her waist. He pulls it back to fish something out of his pocket and stuns Milly by producing a velvet jewelry box. Exactly the right size of box to hold a ring. Staring in shock Milly gasps then turns her surprised face to Daniel who urges her to open the gift.

Carefully lifting up the hinged top Milly's view of the sparkling, solitaire diamond in rose gold is blurred by the happy tears brimming her eyes. "Oh it's so beautiful! Daniel, it's perfect, it's... I'm..." she's too overcome to speak clearly.

"Milly Clarke will you honor me by agreeing to become my wife?" he proposes in a steady, determined voice.

Finding her own she eagerly cries: "Oh yes, yes! Yes, of course I will," she declares. She's surprised to see his shoulders slump in relief, as if he actually doubted what answer she would give.

He carefully slides the ring on the proper finger. A perfect fit and the right size - neither too big nor too small - for her hand. The engagement ring is a top grade diamond that sparkles brilliantly.

Their lips draw them together in another loving kiss. Daniel holds Milly's chin in place while he delivers a deal-sealing kiss that makes her swoony. She blames it on all the excitement of his proposal.

"I finally realized, after all this recent talk about romancing and wooing, that I never did propose to you. I knew I'd left something out and then I panicked about it. I mean, after that magnificent display of temper I couldn't bear the thought of someone else claiming you. It was imperative to act right away and I couldn't wait a moment longer and – oh! Oh no!" he exclaims.

"Oh no, what?"

With a horrified look Daniel says: "Now I have to go into SLO shopping, three days before Christmas, to buy you another present."

Laughing at his dramatics Milly insists he certainly doesn't have to get her anything else.

"Don't argue with me, woman. Christmas morning with nothing under the tree from your fiancé? All the Young men would disown me!" Sighing deeply he goes on: "My fault for not wanting to wait."

"Oh, so there's no ulterior motive to you picking the shortest day of the year to propose?"

"Clever girl, you're right. It's because I want the shortest possible engagement."

Tilting her head Milly asks: "What is a good time of the year for a farmer to get married?"

"Definitely winter, but I don't want to wait a whole year. This town has already had one big Young wedding so I thought maybe we could elope? What do you think?"

"I think people will say your family is against the marriage, they already know I don't have anyone left so the objection would have to come from your side."

Knowing the local gossips really will speculate about that Daniel suggests: "Well then, how about we just have a super small wedding?"

She giggles: "Then they'll say it's a *shotgun ceremony*."

Daniel gives a bad-tempered huff before stating: "Seems to me the townsfolk of Sweet Berry Cove are going to have something to say no matter what we do so why not just please ourselves? We'll get married and they can watch your tummy with their beady eyes anxious to be the first to find scandal."

Milly gives his shoulder a swat but her laugh is a merry gurgle.

Stricken by a thought Daniel exclaims: "Oh! Oh wait a second, Milly did you want a big fancy white wedding? Is that something you've always dreamed about having?"

Before he's finished asking she's shaking her head *no*. "As a girl I figured if I got married it would be just like the weddings I'd grown up hearing about at the commune. I never saw one, the inhabitants were all older people and many of them just lived together, but Sunshine told me not to accept that.

She used to say *married is married and don't let anyone kid you that a license is only a piece of paper, it's a legal document*."

"She was right, it's a serious undertaking as well as being a social convention. Tell me what kind of weddings did they talk about?"

"Oh, hippie weddings! Always outdoors with the whole community attending. Both the women and the men going barefoot and wearing flowers in their hair. Long, floaty dresses and tie-dyed caftans. Waving incense and sage around the couple who would be saying their vows in their own words. Then the bride and groom would each place a string of love beads around the other's neck, pass around a hash pipe, and end the ceremony with a kiss."

There's a telltale crease between Daniel's eyebrows despite him keeping a neutral tone of voice when he asks: "Milly, that's not the kind of wedding you'd like us to have, is it?"

Seeing Daniel's look of utter consternation Milly desperately wants to tease him but fails to keep her expression grave. She can't contain the laughter that bubbles up making him roll his eyes at her.

"Daniel I'm perfectly happy to do whatever is the absolute minimum requirement to make it legal. I would like Reverend Stephen to officiate, preferably in the Church, but just us and um... what about your father for our witness? Unless we need two people?"

"I'll find out the legal stuff, I guess Stephen can help with that. It sounds perfect sweetheart, but do you think we should tell Dad first?"

"No way! I already know your Dad well enough to know he can't keep a secret."

"Oh yeah, you're right about that! but we can tell him we're engaged. We'll tell the whole family. I can't wait to see the looks on everyone's faces at the Christmas party tomorrow night when they see us together and you with this diamond on your ring finger. Dad will probably want to make an announcement."

"Daniel! this is so exciting!" Milly's shining face perfectly reflects her words. "We'll keep our wedding plans a secret, right? When people ask when's the wedding? We'll just be vague about it. We'll set a date ourselves, talk to the Reverend, and then we'll spring it on Samuel at the last minute. You know he'll be disappointed about no reception because he does love a party."

"Who says there won't be a party?"

"Oh we can't, we've already got plenty on the go just now with the holidays–"

"Exactly!" Daniel interrupts. "We're already hosting a New Year's Party so if we can get married that day, on the 31st, we can tell everyone our news that night. That will make it a real celebration to start off 2024."

"And you'll never have to worry about forgetting the date of your anniversary!" Milly quips.

"Tease me all you like now, love, because in ten days you'll be promising God that you'll always love and obey me."

The intense look in his eyes makes Milly shiver in happy anticipation. Daniel's love is so strong Milly truly feels it. She feels how it envelops her in protective warmth and that knowledge, that powerful emotion, is overwhelming. No tricks or games or deception.

For the first time in her life Milly feels worthy because if Daniel loves her, she realizes she must be. And he has earned all her love from the bottom of her heart.

The two of them sit quietly on the rocker-swing enjoying this private space and the profound closeness they feel.

Early Christmas Gift

Last night when Daniel walked upstairs with Milly he gave her a wry smile and a chaste kiss on her forehead. Her eyes sparkled brighter than the diamond on her finger and he was content just to bathe in her happiness. Well, mostly content. She closed her bedroom door and watched underneath it to see the shadow of his feet move away. That didn't happen for a long moment and only after she heard his deep sigh.

Milly couldn't think clearly, her thoughts scattered everywhere darting from one topic to the next, and though she thought she'd never be able to sleep her head hardly touched the pillow and she was out.

At breakfast neither of them said a word of the engagement although Milly flaunted her ring, fluttering her fingers, at every opportunity. Finally Nora shrieked *omigod you're engaged!* grabbing Milly's hand to inspect the diamond and nodding her approval.

"Wait, what? Are you..?" Samuel is wearing a wide happy grin as he sputters to get the words out. Amos calls out *hey! congratulations* just as Esther shouts *I'm your bridesmaid!* Hannah enters the room asking *what's all the noise about?* and when Milly extends her left hand the older woman's frown turns into a smile of delight.

"Oh well done, Daniel. You've got yourself a lovely bride and she'll be a wonderful wife!"

"Son, Milly, what a perfect Christmas present!" exclaims Samuel. "We can let everyone know at the Christmas party this afternoon."

"Actually I was hoping–" Milly turns to Daniel and continues: "that we could go visit Miz Tally and tell her our news first?"

"That's a great idea. I'm sure the news will help brighten her up because she's very fond of you, Milly."

"Well if you're going to go to the hospital you better skedaddle so as you're back in time to head down to the school for the party."

"You're right, Hannah. I'll just clear up these dishes–"

"Never mind about that, Nora and Esther are more than capable," declares the housekeeper staring at the teenager with an expression that won't tolerate excuses.

Milly and Daniel bundle up warmly and head out to the Sweet Berry Cove Care Home.

The receptionist waves them onwards to Miz Tally's room and as they draw closer they're surprised to hear the raised voice of a female mid-argument. Miz Tally's response is too low to decipher but her drawl sounds comfortable enough.

Knocking on the open door Daniel's eyes move from a red-faced, angry Janice Peart to the placid face of her good friend and neighbor.

Hesitantly he asks: "Are we interrupting?" while Milly hangs behind not wanting to intrude.

"Bless you no, dear. Come on in," answers Miz Tally. She's propped up in her bed and even the unfortunate yellow of her crocheted bed-jacket can't drain the healthy color from her cheeks. Her long braid is once again coiled into a crown on top of her head and she looks 100 percent better than she did yesterday morning.

"Maybe Daniel Young can talk some sense into you!" snaps Janice. Although she's a known gossip Janice is generally even-tempered, gathering news to satisfy her curiosity and happily sharing it around. It's unusual to see her so worked up.

"I'm not going to change my mind, Janice. It's kind of you to care, but I'm simply not interested in pursuing it," her friend replies mildly.

"Pursuing what?" asks Milly, stepping forward into the room.

Before answering Miz Tally's sharp eye focuses on Milly's ring finger and the old lady's face is wreathed in smiles as she claps with delight. "Oh my dears, I'm so happy for you. Congratulations and my very best wishes for a long, happy marriage."

Taken aback Janice abandons her argument to demand *what are you talking about? what's going on?*

Milly simply extends her left hand and Janice Peart is momentarily silenced, her mouth forming an O of surprise.

"Well I never... I congratulate you Daniel on being smarter than I credited," is her backhanded compliment. True to her usual script she immediately pushes for news: "When's the wedding?"

"Oh we only got engaged last night so we really haven't established anything, there's no rush," replies Milly.

Daniel notes how Janice Peart's gaze lands on Milly's belly and his eyes briefly narrow as he echoes his fiancée sunnily saying: "No rush at all."

"Oh I just love a happy ending. You two have made an old lady very happy and thank you for coming here to share this news," Miz Tally is her usual sweet self.

"Thank you!" replies Milly. "Now tell me what your doctor is saying because you look wonderful and–"

Interrupting Daniel says: "No, wait before we get into that I want to hear what Janice thinks you should be pursuing?"

Janice doesn't need to be asked twice. "Well, if you can believe it, Tally has the chance to win big money in a lawsuit but she says *she can't be bothered*. Now I ask you..." Her voice trails off in exasperation.

Miz Tally speaks up, more firmly this time, explaining: "The doctors did some forensic investigation – which I thought only happened when someone died – but anyhow, they discovered the source of my sickness. It turns out my Christmas present from Janice, a lovely selection of sourdough loaves, was tainted with that E.coli bacteria."

"Oh no, do they know how that happened? Did lots of people get sick?"

"Ah, this is the fortunate part. The bacteria wasn't in the food, it was transferred to the gift-wrap by an employee who..." she pauses to glance at Daniel then lowering her voice whispers: "A girl who didn't practice proper hygiene after using the restroom. Only traces were transferred to the packaging but that was enough for this frail old senior to fall ill."

"And the bakery has admitted it! They said *we take full responsibility*. They sent their representative all the way up here to meet with Tally and explain what happened, but I say that's not good enough!"

"Oh Janice. It's just one of those things. The employee is a part-time hire for the holiday season and apparently no one else got sick. The man from the bakery apologized so nicely and he's paying all of my hospital bills and gifting me a lifetime supply of their products."

"But I'm telling Tally she should sue. They're a very famous San Francisco bakery, I wouldn't have chosen them otherwise, and they can certainly afford to pay up."

"And as I keep telling you Janice, I don't need the money. Joel left me very well provided for and the bakery didn't do anything wrong. Their employee made a mistake and they've owned up and been very generous. Just look at that big bouquet – it's not flowers, it's fruit! Isn't that something?"

Both Milly and Daniel look at the large display they had mistaken for flowers. Deeply interested Milly moves over to examine it closely.

"How artistic!" she exclaims. "The strawberries are dipped in chocolate that's iced with fancy swirls. The pineapple is cut into daisy shapes with a cherry for the center! Oh, and see how they've scalloped the edge of half-a-watermelon to act as the vase. This is a wonderful thing, it's a great gift!"

Chuckling, Daniel comments in an aside to Miz Tally: "Someone's getting ideas."

Hearing him Milly nods enthusiastically agreeing: "Oh I am! I want to take a couple of photos. And look here, they didn't just get the florist to use a generic *Get Well* card. Hmm, is it a florist who provides these baskets? I guess it could be a florist or maybe a company that only does these fruit arrangements? Ooh! I wonder if they use other foods like chocolate to create bouquets for candy-lovers?

This is a proper card to *Ms. Tallulah Beaumont* with the bakery's logo and signed by several people, they're certainly not trying to downplay their role in this."

"That's 'cause they're guilty," insists Janice.

Ignoring Janice's remark Miz Tallys says: "I believe these fruit flowers are called *edible arrangements*. That's what my nephew said. He and his wife are driving up tomorrow, I'm being discharged into their care, and they'll have me over Christmas but I'll be sure to be back for the Young's New Year's Eve party."

"Oh I'm so glad to hear everything turned out okay," enthuses Milly. "Honestly, this is the best Christmas present ever!"

After visiting for a few more minutes both Milly and Daniel lean in to kiss Miz Tally's cheek. "It's too bad you'll miss the Christmas Party today, that's why we've got to get going now, but we look forward to ringing in another New Year with you, Miz Tally," says Daniel.

Once he and Milly are back in the car he tells her: "Miz Tally's full recovery is second best, and the third best present is that the contaminated food didn't come from our Farm Shop."

"What's the best present?" she asks coyly, biting her lip to hide her smile.

Daniel cocks an eyebrow at her and smirking says: "Why, celebrating Bernie's first Christmas, of course. What else could it be?"

Milly pretends to be annoyed but Daniel pulls across the bench-seat of his old truck holding her close with his arm over her shoulders.

She decides she's too cozy and too comfortable sitting like this to move away to put on her seat-belt. *It's only a short drive,* she reasons as she lays her head against Daniel's chest.

They're fortunate to avoid icy patches on the road and highway patrolmen ready to ticket for infractions.

They don't speak again until Daniel parks the truck and then Milly says, obviously voicing her thoughts aloud, "I know I could do a lot with gingerbread, it's such an easy cookie to shape and decorate, and thick licorice sticks would make great flower stems—"

She's interrupted by Daniel kissing her cheek and murmuring under his breath *I might have known...*

Annual Christmas Party

Traditionally, Sweet Berry Cove's annual Christmas party is an Open House for the whole community. Even though some of the inhabitants are non-Christian, or non-practicing, everyone attends because it's such a fun day.

Held in the school auditorium, the site of the recent Hallowe'en Party, the festivities start mid-afternoon.

The big room has been transformed with the handicrafts of the grade-schoolers. Long, looping chains made from red and green construction paper wreathe the walls and hang in streamers from the ceiling. Artwork depicts winter fun although the students have to rely on imagination since no snow falls in The Cove.

The first item on the program is a combined children's and senior's tea party with entertainment provided by the middle-school choir singing popular holiday songs. Then there's a visit from Santa handing out gaily wrapped presents delivered by giggling middle-school elves. Games of musical chairs are played and all the participants earn goodie bags.

By five o'clock the very young and the very old are flagging and the room hushes into quiet time for naps and dozing. That's when the meal preparation begins. Youths are directed to set-up the trestle tables that are soon covered in colorful Christmas-themed cloths. The same linens are brought out again year after year evoking happy memories from past parties.

Milly is supposed to be working alongside Hannah and Nora but keeps getting waylaid by women noticing her engagement ring and hugging her. Some ask if they've set a date but most assume it will be a fall or winter wedding as is usual for the residents of Sweet Berry Cove.

Milly is noncommittal, simply declaring *it only happened yesterday.* She deflects further questioning by exclaiming: "Isn't that wonderful news about Miz Tally's recovery?"

Everyone agrees and most of them assure Milly that they never believed for a moment that she was in any way responsible. Some don't mention the gossip at all, and the ones who remain suspicious aren't people Milly socializes with anyhow.

Her set-to with Janice Peart is still a hot topic and the consensus is that Milly had every right to speak her mind.

Especially once everyone heard how Doc Watkins lambasted Edie Coulson right in the middle of Michaelson's Pharmacy. The eyewitness to his tirade said *he called her an ignorant, vicious gossip spreading lies!* and her listeners all look suitably shocked. A man adds *that old woman just stood there with her mouth hanging open when he told her there would have been a lot more sick people sick if the problem originated in the Farm Shop.* He spoke as if he'd seen this with his own eyes but he hadn't, it was his wife who'd been in the shop at the time and she'd told him all about it.

As news of this incident makes the rounds people nod knowingly say *makes sense* and *only stands to reason.* They get to indulge in gossip and be righteously judgmental at the same time.

Samuel has broadcast the news of the engagement amongst the men and Daniel is being simultaneously congratulated and commiserated with in the way that males do.

Chris Larch states Daniel has found a real catch and he can say so having sampled Milly's cooking. He knows his wife and Daniel were once engaged but his honest congratulations smooth over any embarrassment between the men.

The ladies of The Cove start setting out the sumptuous banquet of food. A variety of salads and pickled treats lead to bread and buns, vegetable dishes, main entrées of cooked meats, pastas, and fruit. The desserts won't appear for at least another hour to allow everyone to feast and digest.

By time the eating is done the teenagers and young couples are ready to mingle and dance. Milly is utterly entranced watching the line dancing. It seems like everyone, young and old, knows the intricate kicks, hands touching heels, turns, clapping, twisting... it's like some professionally choreographed Hollywood musical with Jim Cairns, Hannah's husband, leading the routines.

When Daniel comes to fetch her to join in Milly refuses, not wanting to look foolish, but she vows to herself that she will learn the dances in time for the New Year's Gala. It's frustrating to sit on the sidelines watching her fiancé charm the ladies with his prowess in the line-dance. Sighing she reminds herself that she's got plenty to keep her busy getting the dessert buffet ready.

Both hot and cold ciders, eggnog, teas, and coffees are offered with the cakes, pies, flans, custards, squares, cookies and cupcakes. The diners chastise themselves *for not leaving enough room to enjoy all these treats!* but they're encouraged to fix up a plate to take home. Milly uses a second paper plate as a cover, writes their name on top, and tapes down the sides.

It's all excellent advertising for the Farm Shop, and for the Shop Café they're opening in the new year.

All the teens are soon back on the make-shift dance-floor and Esther suffers a brief twinge of jealousy seeing Amelia and Simon dancing together. She recalls her talk with Principal Showalty and is able to suppress her envious thoughts.

Besides, it's highly entertaining watching Joanna's attempts to get between those two. Esther and Audrey quirk eyebrows and purse lips into expressions worthy of gossips four times their age and get a great deal of satisfaction out of it.

The local boys put on a show of reluctance but soon Blaine, Andy, and John are two-stepping with the rest of them.

The dancing goes on for a few hours and as the music slows down Milly and Daniel get on the floor along with Amos and Nora and other couples. Samuel, Stephen Smithson, and Peter Showalty take turns dancing with all the women and there are happy smiles all round.

By time the musicians wrap it up the matrons of the community have packed away the leftovers and reclaimed their platters and serving dishes. The school doesn't have suitable facilities for washing up so their husbands will lug it all back home although they won't need to be quite so careful on the return trip. Milly and Nora express delight mixed with guilt once they discover Hannah has taken care of everything from the Young household.

"There's nothing left to do except get all you younger ones off home to your beds. Goodness knows I'm ready for mine!" the housekeeper states.

"As efficient as ever, thank you Hannah," says Samuel, and the rest of the family echo the sentiment.

Dance Lessons

Returning home from the Christmas party the members of the Young household went their separate ways giving Milly and Daniel some alone time.

"Can I tempt you with a mug of steamy cocoa for a nightcap?" she asks archly.

Chuckling at her dramatics Daniel accepts the offer and follows her into the kitchen. Milly prepares their hot drinks with quiet efficiency and Daniel relaxes into the calm environment she creates. His head-to-toe scrutiny is appreciative even though the outfit she's wearing isn't dressy. Milly knew she'd be hands-on with catering and child-minding today so she chose a plain black skirt and a white top patterned with red and green Christmas trees to wear. Daniel is grateful that his competent and practical fiancée is also a lovely young woman. *She's very easy on the eye and I'm a lucky man,* he thinks.

"People were curious about the engagement and asked *when is the wedding?* and *were we out for dinner when you proposed?* and *was I surprised?* and oh my favorite was: *did Daniel go down on one knee?* because I was so tempted to explain you really couldn't since I was sitting in your lap."

"I got plenty of teasing from the men about *the old ball-and-chain* and *another one bites the dust.* Amos was funny saying he always figured he'd have a million gibes for when I *got caught* but because he's such a happy newlywed himself he can't think of thing to joke about. Instead he shook my hand and told me: *marriage, 5 stars, highly recommend.*"

"Aw, that's sweet. Those two are so perfectly suited, you feel their love just by being in the same room. Now there is something I urgently need you to do and by urgent I mean we need to spend a couple of hours on it tomorrow."

"Saturday? What do you need?"

"Jim and Hannah were going to do it but we've never found the time so... it's up to you. You have to teach me how to line-dance before the party on New Year's Eve."

Daniel laughs and agrees, promising Milly will soon be doing a *Grapevine, Apple Jacks*, and a *Kick-Ball Change*. She's mystified and intrigued.

Next day Daniel gets everyone gathered in the sitting-room with the furniture pushed back to leave them plenty of space to dance. Samuel calls out the steps at the regular pace first and then in slow-motion. Amos, Nora, and Esther perform while Daniel and Milly stand behind them and follow along.

"Now Milly I'm an old guy and only know the dances for country and western music. I've heard nowadays they've got some easy line dances for rock 'n roll tunes but I can't teach you those–"

"I can," interrupts Esther, "but they never play the right songs here in The Cove so there's no point."

Patiently waiting until his daughter finishes Samuel continues: "*The Electric Slide* was already popular when I was young and yes, kids, your mother and I did dance to it. The songs have changed but the dance still fits most of them from a disco song called *Electric Boogie* to that popular one by Dwight Yoakum, um..."

"*Fast As You*," answers Amos.

Nodding Samuel says, "That's right! but we're going to learn it to this golden oldie *Achy Breaky Heart*."

Everyone is familiar with the tune and the steps are so simple by the end of the song Milly has picked it up and is performing perfectly.

After practising a few more times Esther moans at her father: "Play something else, Dad. Milly's already got this. See? she's following along without even looking at her feet."

"Okay Esther, how about we teach Milly *Power Jam*. It's got a couple of dozen steps but once you get it down this is a dance you'll do over and over again. In addition to turning and crossovers it's got heel and toe tapping plus a little jump at the end. It's a fun one."

There is much more to learn in this dance and when Milly's wrong turn has her hopping right up into Daniel's chin the group dissolves in laughter.

"Serves you right for standing so close to Milly!" taunts Nora.

"Yeah bro, you don't need to be hangin' on to her hips like that," adds Amos.

Daniel rubs the top of Milly's head to soothe the ache and shushes her apologies for the collision.

Once she's got this dance mastered they all call it quits. Line-dancing gives a good workout despite how casual and easy it looks.

Nora and Amos have a dinner date with friends so Esther begs a ride off them into the village. Samuel tells her he's going to visit Stephen Smithson and she can call him for a ride when she's ready to come home.

Turning to Daniel and Milly he asks if they want to come along but Daniel says *no, I've got to brave the last-minute crowds in SLO tomorrow so I'll be having an early night.*

"Maybe if I can get there as soon as the stores open it won't be too bad."

"Yeah good luck with that, son. The place will be full of men who have no clue what to buy pestering the salesladies for advice and sizes. Why on earth did you leave it to the last second?"

Daniel answers abruptly saying: "Aw it's a long story so I'll tell you another time." Samuel senses his son's embarrassment and tells himself he must remember to follow up and get the whole tale.

To Milly he says: "And what about you Milly? are you happy to stay home on this Saturday night?" in a teasing voice.

Smiling, she reminds him that it's two days to Christmas and since she's got a big dinner planned in addition to their Open House on Boxing Day so there's plenty to keep her busy. Seeing a worried frown appear on his face she's quick to assure Samuel *and I'll enjoy every minute of the preparation.*

"You warned me that The Cove packs in as many celebrations as possible during the slow season and I'm loving every party, dinner, and get-together," she declares happily. "This is my first ever Christmas with a family, you know."

Samuel feels a rush of gratitude at having this lovely young woman be part of his household.

"I'll keep her company, Dad," puts in Daniel.

"Huh! I'm sure you and that dog will be underfoot and getting in my way. I expect I'll be sending you take Bernie out for a walk in less than an hour," Milly retorts. "It'll be the radio playing Christmas music that keeps me company."

Where is Daniel?

Shivering in the cold of early morning Daniel leaves the farmhouse to drive to San Luis Obispo. He wants to be there as soon as the stores open for what he expects will be a busy time on the last shopping day before Christmas. The wind is biting and he's glad of the powerful heater in his old truck.

All of the family are at home and Amelia has been dropped off to visit with her new girlfriend. Making their way to Esther's bedroom snatches of their excited chatter can be heard:

"Amelia, can you line-dance?"

"You do know I'm from West Virginia, right? Oh! I wonder if Simon knows how?"

"Probably not since he comes from San Diego."

Samuel pauses his gift wrapping to greet Amelia, asking if she's ready for Christmas. He likes the girl and is happy his daughter has made a new friend. *I hope her father is able to get her enrolled in Saint Catherine's High with Esther and the other teenagers from The Cove,* he thinks watching the two girls giggling together.

Nora has found another box of Christmas ornaments and ropes Amos into helping her add them to the tree.

"I've got presents to wrap!" he claims.

Nora refuses to accept his excuse stating: "I've already wrapped all the presents for the family."

"Yeah, but I have to wrap your presents–" he begins but she interrupts with an excited grin.

"Presents? Plural?"

"Only because it's our first Christmas as a married couple, don't go thinking this will happen every year," he jokes.

Amos then refuses all her efforts to get him to reveal his secret hiding places. He agrees to help Nora decorate the tree so long as she agrees to give him some privacy afterwards to wrap her gifts *and no peeking!*

Unpacking the box they find it's full of handmade ornaments, products of the Young children's artistic efforts. Amos reminisces about these crafts made out of dough at Sunday school.

"The teacher would take them home to bake and the following week we'd get to paint them. By time it was Esther's turn they had added sparkles so all of these extremely glittery ones are her creations."

"Someone packed them up well."

"That would be Dad. I can't wait to see his face when he spots them on the tree." Turning serious his voice gets emotional as he says: "Thank you Nora, this is a great idea."

Beaming at her husband's praise Nora blows him a kiss before going back to sorting out the pieces for hanging.

Watching how carefully she handles the delicate decorations Amos has a sudden image of a future Nora threading ribbons through their own children's creations. His stillness draws his wife's attention and the look on his face makes her breath catch.

Milly is in her element, happily cooking and baking. Whenever she calls for volunteers to taste-test something fresh out of the oven or to lick the mixing bowl she gets plenty of offers to help. Everyone in the farmhouse is busy with chores and enjoying the spirit of Christmas.

Late in the afternoon Reverend Smithson drops in for a visit knowing there will be freshly baked treats to enjoy. Shortly afterwards Helena and Chris Larch arrive to pick up Amelia. Milly produces coffee, cookies, and cake so they're all gathered round when Stephen tells them he heard on the radio about a bad traffic tie-up on the road to The Cove from SLO.

"Oh no, a car accident? We're headed that way now."

"The news bulletin asked people to stay away from the area, in fact to stay off the roads if possible, but it didn't say why."

Everyone realizes Daniel has been gone far longer than expected and no one has heard from him. Samuel immediately dials his mobile but gets the automated message *the party you are trying to reach is not available, please try again later.*

"No signal, I guess."

Nora frets saying: "Daniel is such an accident-prone man–"

Helena interrupts exclaiming "What? Since when? He was never clumsy, he was always very athletic."

Amos replies: "Ah, but that sure changed. Just in the past four or five months he's chopped his arm with an ax so bad he needed stitches, then he got trampled on by George–"

"George is our bull," Samuel explains in an aside to Chris.

"But all that is Milly's fault," says Esther artlessly. When everyone stares she says "Well obviously not on purpose, sheesh! but because he was too busy thinking about Milly instead of paying attention to what he was doing."

"Oh! That's quite astute little sister."

"Huh! I'm not stupid. And Milly's had a couple of scrapes herself first with the rumors and then almost drowning."

"Drowning? What's that all about?" Stephen Smithson and the Larches hadn't heard about that incident and they turn to Milly to explain.

"Oh it's embarrassing, it was awfully silly on my part. I thought I was rescuing Bernie from the tide coming in but he swam back to shore and I ended up getting stranded on a rock. It wasn't that far out but I don't know how to swim. Luckily Daniel spotted me and came to the rescue. I was already in the water by then and panicking but he's an expert swimmer and got us both safely back to land. He's going to teach me how to swim come summer."

With a deep frown Stephen demands: "How come I never heard about this?" but there's no answer to that.

Milly asks Samuel: "Can we put on the Weather Channel and see if that tells us anything?"

"Good idea! now where's that remote?"

Nora finds the device and clicks to the appropriate channel. They join the program catching the weatherman in mid-sentence announcing:

"...a freak ice storm. Freezing rain due to the sudden drop in temperatures has caused sections of Routes 1 and 101 to close. The strong winds have polished the road surface and black ice is sending cars skidding in every direction. There are several pile-ups. A tractor-trailer has jackknifed and a couple of semis overturned haphazardly blocking lanes in all directions. Emergency vehicles are on scene with ambulances called for medical issues but no fatalities reported. To repeat, our top story is a freak ice storm—" Samuel mutes the TV but leaves it on.

"Well... I guess that's good news," says Milly doubtfully.

"I will pray for everyone to return safely home to their families," adds Stephen. From some people that might sound sanctimonious but the sincerity of the Reverend's faith shines through in an aura of goodwill. The Youngs takes comfort in his words.

"Hon, I think you better call your mother and see if she can put us up for tonight. I know it'll be a squeeze, but..."

Helena makes a quick call and after she finishes tells them: "Well that's worked out well. Mom is absolutely thrilled to have us there for Christmas morning."

The Calvary Church doesn't hold a midnight mass but there is an evening service at 9:00 that's popular with the villagers who enjoy singing carols along with the choir. Samuel urges the Larch family to go with Stephen to the church, promising to text once they have news. The four of them leave, each assuring the other that *everything will be fine.*

Christmas Eve often feels like a long night to get through and tonight is no exception. Instead of excitement and happy anticipation keeping them awake it's unspoken anxiety. It's too early to go to sleep anyhow.

The family members sit with their worries to a background of pop Christmas music playing on the radio.

"Amos you got to know that State Trooper quite well, right?"

"Barry Merkel? Oh yeah, we spoke several times and... oh! you think I should call him for news? good idea, hon!"

Amos scrolls through the contacts on his phone until he finds the number and calls. He puts the phone on speaker and the company relaxes when Trooper Merkel answers *Hello, Amos* in a cheery voice.

"Barry, I know you've got to be busy tonight but we were wondering–"

"Ah, you've heard the doom-and-gloom on the TV news, huh? Well there's nothing for you to worry about. Yes, we've got lots of vehicles stuck out here on the highway but all the surrounding counties have sent out truckloads of sand so we're gradually clearing lanes and getting the road driveable again.

That brother of yours, what a character! He's got this ancient pick-up truck that just won't quit and he's hauling cars out of the ditch and even helping get the big trucks right-side up. He claims *it's because the old beater has no tech and is manual-everything* so he's managing where late model SUVs are just spinning round and round."

The whole family is grinning happily at the good news and giving each other knowing grimaces at the mention of Daniel's old pick-up truck.

"Anyhooo we should all be heading home soon. Spirits are good, people are sharing goodies they bought for the holidays, and most folks have travel mugs of coffee and water bottles so everyone is getting some nourishment."

"They said something about ambulances on the news?"

Trooper Merkel puts their minds at ease explaining in his chatty way: "Oh we did have one asthma attack that got fixed up with oxygen, from the fire truck actually, and one poor old soul slipped on the ice landing on his ankle but it's a sprain not a break. Of course the paramedic said a break would be less painful but a sprain will heal much faster. Frankly, it's a real-life Christmas miracle that no one was seriously injured and most of these cars are able to drive out of the mess."

After many thanks and *Merry Christmas* wishes Amos ends the call with a heartfelt sigh of relief that all will be well. "Milly I can't believe you actually drove that old monster of Daniel's."

"I learned to drive on a truck like that," she answers. Then, to everyone's surprise and most of all herself, Milly bursts into tears. Nora rushes over to embrace and comfort the younger woman who keeps saying *it's such a relief* and *I don't know why I'm crying*.

Samuel asks Esther if she wouldn't mind texting her friend Amelia to pass on the good news, saying he'll do the same with Stephen who is no doubt busy with his parishioners right now.

"Well I think I should get this girl to bed," declares Nora but Milly stubbornly insists that she won't be able to sleep and would much rather wait up until Daniel gets home.

"I'm going to thaw some of the soup I put in the freezer and have it warming on the stove. I'm sure he'll be chilled to the bone by time he gets in."

"What kind of soup did you make?" asks Amos, but Nora gives him a swat saying "You've been filling up on nuts and chips and baked goods all day and night so you don't need to eat another thing. There's going to be lots and lots of food over the next few days so you better leave some room!"

Amos chuckles in agreement and giving Milly a hug says: "If you get too lonely, or too worried, just knock on our door and we'll come keep you company."

"Thanks, Amos but I'm sure I'll be fine."

It's another two hours later when a chilled, tired, and hungry Daniel Young arrives back home. The farmhouse is the only building showing lights for miles around and it's such a welcome sight. Even more welcoming is the delicious aroma of some homemade broth that greets him the moment he opens the door.

He follows his nose to the kitchen where he finds his bride-to-be curled up in the old overstuffed armchair sound asleep with Bernie spilling out of her lap and a colorful quilt haphazardly covering them both.

Daniel feels a calming warmth infuse his whole being at this picture of domestic bliss. The sight of Milly sleeping peacefully brings out a need to protect, love, and care for her. Seeing the table set for his late meal shows she has the same instinctive need to look after him.

The dog doesn't bark but his tail wags wildly when his master appears. Milly wakens then and yawning hugely sees her fiancé and exclaims *Daniel! thank heaven, you're home safe and sound.*

He gives his assurance that he'll always come home to her. Dropping a kiss on his sleepy girl he scoops her in his arms to carry up the stairs. Depositing a protesting Milly on her bed he insists she go back to sleep saying *I'm perfectly capable of serving myself a bowl of soup.*

Straightening up he continues: "Thank you for having that ready for me, sweetheart. I'm starving! Besides, if I know Dad he'll soon appear downstairs just to ease his mind that I'm okay. Good night, and when you wake up in the morning we'll have a wonderful Christmas together."

Murmuring her agreement through a yawn Milly snuggles into her pillow while Daniel looks on fondly.

Christmas Day

Now that she's almost seventeen Esther is trying her hardest to be cool about Christmas but she can't withstand Milly's enthusiasm. It's infectious, contagious, and irresistible. Everyone is sitting comfortably around the Christmas tree except Milly who is kneeling among the presents happily finding gifts to hand out to everyone.

Milly woke early. After hours of apprehension and worry on Daniel's behalf the relief of having him safely home sent her into a sound sleep. She faintly remembers him carrying her upstairs while she struggled to keep her eyes open. He put her to bed like a beloved child, warm and secure in the safety of his care.

"Samuel! this is for you," she says passing the man a brightly wrapped box. Before he's even begun opening it she's searching out something for a different recipient.

"Nora, look! This has such pretty paper and what a fancy bow on it!" Nora is handed a small professionally decorated package. Her eyes fly to meet Amos's and they share a happy smile.

Esther scrambles down from her seat on the ottoman and shoves an inquisitive Bernie out of the way promising to find something for him. She rummages around but keeps finding gifts for herself that she piles to one side.

"Here, this one says *to Bernie from Santa*," giggles Milly. Daniel rolls his eyes but he can't contain his grin. Esther takes the bone-shaped item from her and holds it for Bernie to chew the wrapping off.

The smell of the rawhide treat has his tail wagging like a metronome set at maximum speed. He bats it out of Esther's hands and possessively traps it between his front paws, happily gnawing.

"Oh Amos!" Nora exclaims. She holds up a beautiful gold bangle studded with colorful gemstones for everyone to admire. "It's beautiful and I love it!"

"Well, I figure with all those different colors you can wear it with most of your clothes."

"I will wear it every day," she promises, leaning over to give him a kiss. "Thank you so much, it's wonderful."

"And here's a present for Amos from Nora," says Milly.

Amos reaches to take the gift bag filled with festive tissue paper and ribbons. He's noticed Nora anxiously biting her bottom lip and resolves to say *I love it* no matter what but when he sees his present he doesn't have to feign delight. "A HIFI WALKER! Nora love, this is fantastic!"

"Really? I'd never heard of them but the salesman assured me any audiophile will love it."

"He's right, it's perfect. Look it's lossless with DAC input and–" he breaks off to pull her into a grateful hug.

"I know Sony Walkman is the top player but I'm afraid my teacher's salary doesn't stretch that far," she states.

"No really this is perfect for me. I can carry it everywhere without constantly worrying it's going to fall and get cracked or even break, not like I would with something super-expensive. No, this is exactly what I want, and I will use it all the time."

Loudly clearing her throat Milly interrupts announcing: "Here's one for you, Daniel. It's from your Dad. And Esther, your gifts are piling up so you better start opening them."

Samuel says: "Esther hand something to Milly, she hasn't opened anything yet."

Esther looks at the stack of gifts still waiting distribution and finds a bulky, awkwardly wrapped package. "Here Milly, this is for your from... oh! it says *love, Bernie.*" They all look at Daniel who shrugs his shoulders but can't hide his smile. He's surprised at the way Milly tears the paper off the gift basket. He'd imagined she'd be the type to carefully unwrap, fold, and save the paper for next year.

Laughing she exclaims: "Oh look! Bernie must be hinting that I stink because he's given me all these lovely scented gifts. There's a bunch of different bath-soaps, *Romance by Ralph Lauren* perfume - ooh, I bet that was expensive - and mmm, honeysuckle bubble-bath. I'm gonna smell so good!"

They all join in the laughter and continue opening presents while smiling and modeling and thanking each other. Memories of past holidays are shared and the atmosphere is one of love and contentment.

Milly has never experienced a family event like this Christmas morning and her heart feels full to bursting. She's so happy and warmed by the love the Youngs have for each other and now for her too. She's found a home at last.

Her lips tremble with emotion and her eyes shine with happy tears. Daniel lifts her onto his lap and rubs soothing circles on her back. Each family member finds the picture the two of them make heartwarming. The aura of goodwill and love continues to permeate the room.

Someone's tummy rumbles and Milly breaks the spell jumping to her feet saying: "Breakfast coming right up!" as she dashes to the kitchen.

The rest of the day continues just as pleasantly. Milly is in her element serving platters of festive treats. Holiday-decorated cookies, iced gingerbread men, butter tarts, coconut bars, and brownies to eat; with foamy egg-nog, frothy hot chocolate, and mulled cider warmed to bring out its spicy aromas to drink.

New books are opened, new music tracks are played, and throughout it all they hear the squeak-squeak of Bernie's toy football, his present from Esther.

Today is just for the family while tomorrow they host an Open House. This Boxing Day tradition goes back through generations of the Johansen family who originally invited neighbors to enjoy a traditional Scandinavian smorgasbord of hot and cold fish, meat, and cheese dishes.

"Milly, I was telling Amelia about you growing up in a hippie commune and she thought that was so cool. She asked what you did for Christmas back then but I didn't know so how did you celebrate?"

"Oh Christmas was always fun but Sunshine told me they considered it *merely a secular holiday*. Everyone in the community had an opinion with most saying they no longer believed in organized religion so there were never any kind of religious ceremonies at holidays like Christmas or Easter.

They were ex-Christian or ex-Jewish, some lapsed Catholics who explained you never stop being Catholic, quite a few atheists, while Buddhism and Bahá'í were both very popular."

"I've heard of the Bahá'í Faith but never met anyone who practiced it," states Nora.

"Oh well from what I could tell it's a lot like Buddhism except that's very old and Bahá'í is only like 150 years old or something like that. I was told all about it but pretty much all I remember is that it's belief in one God - although He's called by many names - harmony and peace, and acceptance of others.

I'm sure I told you before that Sunshine joined all the local churches to get the free social programs they offered for Seniors. She was always busy, very active, and I think... hmm... I think she told me her family was Jewish, but I'm not positive."

Esther is almost belligerent when she states: "But you're Christian, aren't you?"

Milly doesn't react to the teen's tone of voice as she mildly agrees that Esther is correct.

"Esther don't you remember it was Milly's minister from her Calvary Church that told her about the job here?" asks Amos.

"I almost joined the Anglican Church but..." here Milly breaks off shaking her head with a smile. "I was too young. It was a High church and at age twelve I was in love with the rituals but the one Sunshine took me to didn't allow confirmands under fourteen. Huh! I'm surprised I still remember that word.

By time I reached that age Sunshine and I had added the Calvary Church to our rotation and from the very first service there everything just felt right for me.

Anyhow, the point of all this is to say our Christmas celebrations weren't religious although the Wiccans did follow some pagan rituals–"

"Wiccans? As in witches?" interrupts Daniel.

"Uh yes, they were, but the good kind. The kind who brewed medicinal potions and bagged herbs for protection from the evil eye, or to have good luck in romance. They never practised *black magic* because they said *that's always returned threefold.*

The Wiccans celebrated the Winter Solstice, they called it Yule, so the commune started the holiday on December 21st and it lasted past New Year's. It was pretty much just feasting and dancing and exchanging handmade gifts. Sunshine told me it was much better now that they'd all gotten older. They way she hinted I think it was practically an orgy back when they were young."

Waggling his eyebrows at Nora Amos teases: "Hey hon, maybe we should convert?"

"Don't let Stephen hear you!" his wife retorts. Turning to Milly she says: "Don't mind Amos, continue with what you were telling us."

"That's about it. It was fun and we all looked forward to it, in fact the preparation leading up to the holiday was a major part of it. I guess that's normal when the gifts have to be whittled or knit or woven, everything made by hand—"

"Like what?" Nora is curious.

"Oh, let's see what gifts I remember getting," she pauses to think for only a moment before her face lights up with a smile. "I got this beautifully carved cradle that actually rocked and it came with a rag-doll wearing a matching dress and bonnet, and a sock monkey, sachets of scented herbs for wardrobe and dresser drawers, oh right I was given this tweed cape that one of the women homespun that I loved so much. I wore it till it literally fell apart years later.

The community was determined to avoid all the commercialism of Christmas they claimed happened in the outside world but I had no experience of that. All I know is Sunshine always made sure I had a good holiday and it's times like these that I really miss her, but I have lots of good memories."

It appears that Esther is still having trouble with the concept of Sunshine's version of religion.

"But if your Guardian went to a whole bunch of churches then she must have been super-religious, right? but from you said it doesn't sound like she was."

"Sunshine also found that the Calvary Church answered, or satisfied, something inside her. She didn't lump it with the other religions and for the last few years of her life those were the only services she attended. She's buried in the churchyard."

Turning to Daniel Milly says: "I sent an email to Reverend Johnson saying I would like to arrange for Sunshine's headstone. Now that I've got my inheritance I didn't want to waste a moment to get things in motion. I sent an email to Matt Ellison as well, asking if he thinks we should use Sunshine's real name or her chosen one."

Interested in the answer Daniel asks: "What did he say?"

"He hasn't replied yet, or maybe he has but I haven't been online today so I wouldn't know."

"Okay, my curiosity is piqued," says Nora and Samuel nods in agreement.

"Oh that's right, you weren't there. We had this discussion with Helena at the Farm Shop," says Daniel. After thinking a moment he adds: "You know she's a different person when her husband's around... much nicer and more relaxed or something."

"I noticed that too," puts in Milly. "Chris is a good influence and they're happy together."

"Mmm, well back when we had this conversation Helena was definitely *not* impressed when you explained how you wanted to give Sunshine a headstone, was she?"

Chuckling at the memory Milly says: "No, she sure wasn't. I think she was hoping I'd say I wanted a designer wardrobe with plenty of jewelry and expensive shoes."

"With matching handbags, of course!" puts in Nora.

"Oh, naturally," Milly agrees.

"I shouldn't make fun of Helena, I quite like her," Nora admits.

"I think we all like *Mrs. Larch*," Amos specifies.

When dinnertime comes around everyone is groaning that they're *too full to eat another bite* until Milly starts ferrying plates already made up with turkey and stuffing, mashed potatoes and gravy, and thick ham with a choice of mustard or hot honey sauces.

In between mouthfuls Nora complains: "Milly, you're killing us. We're all going to need to go on starvation diets come the New Year."

"Just eat what you can and leave the rest, but of course if you want seconds there's still plenty more in the kitchen. I fixed up the plates in there because I'm using the rest of the bird to make up a couple of the dishes for tomorrow. I'm not doing a lot of savory food, everyone will have had their own Christmas feasts, but cold cuts with fancy breads and cheese are always popular."

"And no doubt there will be a ton of desserts full of calories!" laughs Daniel.

"Millions of them," Milly assures him.

They manage to find enough appetite to enjoy their Christmas dinner. Before Milly brings out the dessert selection they're interrupted by a ringing phone. Samuel frowns at Esther but she pulls her mobile from her pocket saying *it's not mine.*

"It's mine!" exclaims Nora in surprise. "Who could be calling me at dinnertime on Christmas Day?"

"You better answer it, hon. It might be..." Amos doesn't finish and his face shows a worried frown.

Nora hurries back into the sitting room to find her cellphone and they hear her anxious *hello?* before she happily cries out "Dad! Yes, a very merry Christmas to you, too!"

Amos glances round the table sharing his relief that the call isn't bad news. They can all hear Nora excitedly questioning her father and then laughing and talking with her half-siblings. This is practically unheard-of since Nora's stepmother is notoriously jealous. It's a wonderful occurrence, especially at the holidays.

The call doesn't last long and before rejoining the family Nora hurries to the restroom to wipe away the evidence of her happy tears. Taking her seat she beams a smile so wide her cheeks must be aching. Amos reaches over to give her hand a squeeze.

Esther now announces: "The next tradition we have is watching a couple of Christmas movies." She produces a selection of holiday DVDs and the adults simply agree with her choices. It's guaranteed they'll all nod off digesting the day's big meals.

Although she struggles to keep this wonderful day going forever eventually even Milly loses the battle against her drooping eyelids. When Bernie wakens them with an urgent woof she happily snuggles back into the warm spot Daniel leaves when he gets up to let the dog out.

Coming back into the room Daniel pauses for a moment to survey his family. He feels such love and pride for every one of them. Esther sitting on a big cushion on the floor leaning against Samuel's legs, Nora curled up on her husband's lap, and Milly hogging his spot on the love-seat. Enjoying the aromatic warmth of the apple wood fire Daniel concludes that life is good and they are very lucky people.

Samuel's eyes open and catching Daniel's gaze he winks and leans down to stroke his daughter's hair. Esther wakes up with a yawn exclaiming she's past due calling Amelia and heads off to her bedroom. The rest of them stir with Amos taking Nora to their room and Daniel chasing Milly off to her bed advising: "You'll have another early start tomorrow so get your beauty sleep now, sweetheart."

Sleepily she smiles agreeing that she'll be busy tomorrow. "Daniel, Samuel, today was just... just perfect. I had the best time of my life."

"Oh Milly, you made it wonderful for the whole family and I thank you for that. We will all look forward to many more happy Christmases in the years ahead."

"That's right hon, you did a great job. Now, go get tucked in. Dad and I will stay up for a bit," says Daniel.

"Good idea son, I could go for a game of cribbage."

"Do you want me to make a pot of tea for you two?"

"No!" they both chorus. "You go to your bed and leave us to see to ourselves. Good night, Milly."

Daniel walks with her to the bottom of the stairs. Enfolding her in a loving embrace his mouth finds hers in a tender yet passionate kiss. The small sigh that escapes her lips makes Daniel groan with the whispered promise of *only a few more days.*

Bernie Gets Sick

Samuel has just set out the cribbage board and cards when Bernie lets loose with a loud and long howl followed by pitiful yips.

"Uh-oh, that doesn't sound good," says Samuel sharing a concerned look with Daniel who agrees and they hurry out to the boot room. They're greeted by a foul odor and liquid messes spewing out of the pup from both ends.

"He must have eaten something bad!" shouts Daniel, rushing to kneel by the dog. "His heart is going a mile a minute and look how the poor guy is shaking."

Amos rushes in behind them but stops Nora from following when he realizes the dog is in a very bad way. "I'll call the vet," he begins but Nora interrupts saying "The clinic is closed today, I'll call Luisa at home." She runs back to their room to get her phone and already has her friend, Dr. Bautista, on speaker when she returns.

"Daniel, any idea what he had?" asks the vet.

"No, but he's got the shakes and he's peeing, pooping, and vomiting all at the same time," explains Daniel with a catch in his voice.

The vet calmly instructs them to bundle up the dog warmly and bring him straight to the clinic, she'll be waiting for them.

Dr Luisa Bautista operates her veterinary clinic in a large compound that also houses her trailer-home along with separate boarding kennels for both cats and dogs.

Amos sorts through the blankets on Bernie's dog bed but they're sodden. Grabbing a knitted quilt off the rocking chair he gently wraps up the shivering dog. Daniel has run to get the truck and he's now pulled up to the kitchen door.

Hearing all the commotion Milly arrives and is able to enlighten them saying: "Oh poor Bernie, and to think I was so mad at him when he got into my baking supplies."

"What? When was this?"

"And what did he get into?"

"Everything! I found him in the pantry with his paws white from flour and his face nose-deep in the cocoa powder. He'd torn the bag wide open and was happily chowing down. I told him he was a naughty dog, the mess was everywhere, and after wiping his paws I chased him out."

"Cocoa powder? Chocolate?"

"Yes, that too. There's nothing left of my supply of baker's chocolate which is surprising because it's so bitter–"

"Bitter? Why, is it dark chocolate?"

"Yes, of course. There's no sugar in it, it's unsweetened–" Milly explains but Daniel has already raced off in the old truck after shouting to Nora to tell the vet.

The two women look at each in confusion saying *what?* and *why?* but Amos interrupts urgently asking: "When did this happen, Milly? Nora, get Luisa on the phone again."

"Oh, um, I caught Bernie in there about 1:00 or so? Remember no one wanted lunch at noon so it would have been about an hour later when I went in to the kitchen to fetch snacks."

"Luisa? It's Nora again. Daniel's on his way but he wanted us to tell you that Bernie ate dark chocolate – baker's chocolate – and chocolate powder, I mean cocoa."

"Oh no, when? and how much?"

"We think it was about eight hours ago."

Milly joins the conversation saying: "Dr Luisa he ate quite a lot and it's all my fault. I've been baking so much that I just left everything on the shelves instead of putting it away in the cupboard. It looks like he's emptied his stomach so he'll be okay, won't he?"

The vet neatly sidesteps answering Milly's question saying: "I've got to go, I can see the lights of Daniel's truck now." And she ends the call.

Milly bursts into tears and Nora feels ready to join her. Amos offers to clean up the mess in Bernie's area so Samuel shepherds the women back to the sitting-room.

"Did you not know that chocolate is poisonous to dogs, Milly?" he asks, but in a gentle, non-accusatory tone of voice.

Tearfully she shakes her head *no* and Nora also remarks: "I had no idea either. What's wrong with chocolate?"

"There are chemicals in it that affect dogs' brains. Cats, too."

"Oh no, I never knew that!"

"Well you wouldn't, I guess, if you've never had a pet. It's not your fault, but Bernie... well, I'm afraid it's very serious so prepare yourself, girls."

Milly takes a deep breath and announces: "I'm getting dressed and I'll head out there now." Samuel's kindly face is lined with worry as he tries to dissuade her but Milly insists: "I don't want Daniel to have to face this alone."

Nora says she'll go help Amos and the three of them separate. When Milly has changed and come down the stairs she finds Samuel in his overcoat waiting for her. He leads her out to his car which is running with the heater on high.

The two of them are silent on the journey, wrapped up with their own thoughts. It's a short trip and they can see the clinic lights well before they reach the turn-off. A far-off sound of barking dogs greets them when they pull into the yard, it sounds like the kennel is full for the holidays. Milly and Samuel hurry inside and are startled at the number of people present.

"We were having an *Orphan's Dinner*," states Stephen Smithson explaining that Luisa graciously hosted Christmas dinner for the Cove inhabitants who are on their own for the holiday.

"Stephen had us at Thanksgiving, and it will be my turn at Easter," adds Peter Showalty.

"Oh! You would have been more than welcome–" and "We would have been happy–" say Samuel and Milly speaking at the same time but Sandy Sunday puts up her hand to stop them.

"We each had plenty of invitations but none of us like to gatecrash a family event. Oh I know you're going to say it would be no bother but really, this suits us better."

"It's no time to indulge in one of our theological debates, Samuel, but I am praying for Bernie's recovery even if I'm not sure whether or not I believe dogs have souls."

Samuel smiles at his friend and thanks him for his prayers. "I guess Daniel is in there with Luisa?"

"Yes, he wouldn't leave the poor pup and Bernie couldn't take his eyes off his master."

"From what we've overheard it seems he had quite a bit more than just the chocolate in his stomach and apparently that has helped."

Milly looks doubtful saying: "Well, I know he had some flour but that's not an emetic..."

"I think Luisa meant there were other foods to help dilute the effects, or maybe just to have other items to be sick with? frankly I'm not going to ask for clarification," Peter puts in earnestly.

"It's awfully quiet in there now," states Sandy and the five of them look towards the examining room.

Less than a minute later a white-faced Daniel pushes through the swing-door and seeing everyone gathered he exhales a deep sigh of relief saying: "Luisa says he's gonna be okay."

Everyone comments happily at the news and Milly goes to Daniel taking hold of both his hands. "I am so, so sorry Daniel. I had no idea about chocolate harming dogs–"

Daniel pulls her into his arms and hugs tightly saying: "I know you didn't know, sweetheart. It's not your fault. If anything it's on me because I should have warned you. I know you've never owned a dog before."

Dr. Luisa comes through the doorway pulling down her mask. She exudes calm satisfaction telling them: "I'm keeping him in tonight, he's on a drip, but I'm confident we've passed the danger point. It's good you got him to me so quickly, Daniel."

"What's good is that you were here to take care of him. Thank you so much, Luisa."

"Yes doctor, thank you, thank you so much! We're so sorry to have put you to this trouble."

"Well I'm guessing there won't ever be a repeat performance of this kind of episode but you've got an active puppy who is curious and nosey and always ready to eat so, be prepared for more upsets in the future. Just not this bad, huh?"

"Can we see him before we go?" asks Milly.

"Better not. He's sedated now and I've turned the lights down so he can rest easily."

"What time should I come by tomorrow to pick him up?"

"I'll phone you to confirm but now that the chocolate has been purged out of his system he really should be completely fine after a good sleep."

"Thank you again, we really owe you."

"I'll send you a bill for the medications but the rest is no charge, we'll call it your Christmas present," the doctor adds with a chuckle.

"Oh yes, *Merry Christmas everyone!*"

The three of them are invited to stay and visit for awhile, which Samuel accepts, but Milly and Daniel say *no thanks* and ride back home in his truck. Daniel had opened the windows en route and forgot about them when he hurried in to the clinic. The interior of the truck is very cold but at least any lingering smell of sick dog has been blown away. The heater is soon blasting out warmth.

Daniel is quietly worrying about Bernie but when the road curves sending moonlight shining into the front seat he's remorseful at seeing Milly's miserable expression. Reaching to clasp her hand he tugs her as close as the seat-belt allows.

"Milly, sweetheart, it's not your fault. That's down to me for not alerting you, right? Remember I said I'd work with you on dog training? Well that would have been one of our lessons, we just never got around to it. So you can't blame yourself, that's like blaming Bernie–"

Interrupting she insists: "It's not his fault! he's just a dog."

"Exactly. He's a perfectly normal dog which means he's naughty, greedy, and curious."

"Oh but if I'd only–"

"Uh-uh, now it's my turn to interrupt. The phrase *if only* is sad and useless. It's no good wishing facts away, and regrets don't help unless we learn from them. We left Bernie unattended long enough for him to get into mischief in the pantry, but that's not the only way he could have gotten chocolate. Maybe you'd have given it to him as a treat if he begged for it because no one told you it was bad for him."

"Well I certainly won't do that now that I know."

"Exactly. We all learned something tonight and our boy came through it like a champ and he'll be okay. Luisa is an excellent vet and we're lucky to have her close by."

Relieved by Daniel's reassurances Milly relaxes enough to give him a small smile. He smiles back noticing, now that his worries about his dog have been settled, just how sweetly pretty she looks. He gives her hand another squeeze happily thinking *she's adorable!*

Boxing Day Open House

Hannah is back at work after two day's off. Breakfast is laid out early and she's encouraging everyone to *fix your plate, eat up, and then get out of the way*. She's planned a thorough dust, polish, and vacuuming before the guests arrive for this afternoon's Open House.

When Milly relates the story of Bernie getting into the baking chocolate Hannah comments: "Poor pup, but at least now I can run the vacuum without him barking his head off."

Milly thinks the Saint Bernard's near-death experience deserves more sympathy but Hannah has already armed herself with cleaning supplies and zeal.

Nora comes into the kitchen talking on her phone. Ending the call she asks: "Where's Daniel? That was Luisa on the phone calling to say she'll bring Bernie back with her when she comes to the party. Saves him making the trip to the clinic."

"Good, I've got work for him and Amos. I need the couches pushed back and more chairs brought into the sitting room. They can bring in the dining-room chairs too since people won't be sitting at the table."

"Hannah, I don't think we'll need a lot of seating," says Nora. "People don't visit for long at an Open House. They'll just have a hot drink and a plate of goodies and talk about their Christmas for an hour or so."

"Huh! Don't kid yourself, girls. Verna and Myrna Harrigan will arrive early, park themselves on a couch, and they'll be the last to leave. That Janice Peart will tag along with them. She'll be at a loose end with Miz Tally down south at her nephew's place."

"Oh! That's really not the point of... oh well, you know our neighbors much better than I do so I'm sure you're right."

"I am, but don't you worry about them overstaying their welcome because Jim and I will shift them when it's time to call it a day. Now, let's find those boys and get this room sorted."

"No rush, Hannah, we've invited people to come by starting at 2:00 pm–"

"They'll be here at 1:00 to make sure they get the most comfortable seats," the older woman asserts.

As she goes in search of the men Nora widens her eyes making a surprised face at Milly who fights back a giggle. She would never offend their housekeeper, Hannah has been incredibly kind to her from the first moment she arrived at the Young's farmhouse.

Sure enough the doorbell rings and the front door is opened at 1:03. No one locks their doors in The Cove during the day and Janice Peart's voice echos through the hallway calling: "Hello? Happy Boxing Day! Can we come in?" as she enters followed by the Harrigan sisters, Sweet Berry Cove's librarians.

Rolling her eyes Hannah grimaces at Milly as they head out to the hallway to greet the early arrivals.

Samuel is there taking coats which he passes to Esther to carry upstairs to his bedroom. It's certain that all the ladies will need to visit the restroom before they head home so they can get their outdoor clothes at the same time.

Hannah has shut the bedroom doors but only after making sure the rooms passed her inspection. She knows a closed door won't deter nosey visitors from poking their heads in for a quick look round.

The three guests get comfortably settled and begin their questioning by asking after Bernie. Milly is amazed they've heard about last night's emergency trip to the vet but Hannah isn't at all surprised.

Someone would have remarked on having seen Daniel's truck racing along the road on Christmas night, while someone else would comment about how they'd been surprised to see lights on in the veterinary clinic when it was supposed to be closed, and speculation would connect the dots. The gossips considered themselves latter-day Miss Marples who enjoyed deducing answers more than being told facts.

As the party progresses everyone commiserates about poor Bernie and it's a relief to inform them that *happily he will recover fully*. Janice Peart comments *lots of close calls lately* but Milly quells her with a look.

The ladies are holding court and greeting each new arrival with intense interest. Nora mutters under her breath *step into my parlour said the spider to the fly*. Milly doesn't know the poem or that Nora has misquoted the opening line but she understands the sentiment.

Upon seeing Janice Peart the guests ask after Miz Tally, anxious to know how the popular elderly lady is doing. Janice is Miz Tally's good friend and neighbor so they expect her to have the answers.

"Tally is much frailer than she likes folks to know. For awhile it was touch-and-go and if I hadn't insisted Doc Watkins call the ambulance immediately, well..." she breaks off, her expression grim.

A chorus of *oh how dreadful, what a blessing you were there* and *you probably saved her life* is gratifying and Janice accepts it all as her due. "What really bothers me is knowing they're going to get away with it, with poisoning and almost killing her."

Now the audience is rapt, hanging on every word. Everyone has heard that baked goods were the culprit but where they originated is unclear.

"I told her she should sue them for all they put her through. It stands to reason that the bakery producing world-famous San Francisco sourdough would pay a pretty penny to protect its reputation. But Tally is so stubborn. I warned her she might have complications later on and she shouldn't be shortsighted."

Several women nod in agreement with one stating: "You're right, Janice. I've heard of cases where things took a turn for the worse afterwards."

Phrases from background whispers of *came from San Francisco* and *it wasn't our Farm Shop* and *I could have told you that!* can be heard from the audience.

"It's not right that they won't pay up," says another,

"Oh they gave her something and paid all the medical expenses—"

She's interrupted by indignant cries of *I should hope so* and *that's the least they could do!*

Pausing dramatically Janice muses: "Maybe I should be the one to sue the bakery? It was me who actually bought the tainted product."

Nora tactfully states: "I think you have to prove you've suffered physically or financially in order to bring a suit."

"Huh! Some sharp city lawyer can get around something like that easy enough," retorts Janice.

"Maybe... but hiring them might cost a lot of money."

"No, they do it on spec and then take a large chunk of the award settlement—" chimes in one of the Harrigan sisters.

"If that's ever actually paid out," warns the other.

"That's true! It's a scandal how people can win the judgment but never see any money."

"You can bet the lawyers get paid, though."

A new batch of guests are understandably confused at what they've walked in on so Amos loudly changes the subject by asking *did you have your Christmas dinner at home? or were you out with friends?*

The talk turns back to yesterday's celebrations and it seems everyone has a funny, happy story to relate. The visitors who brought their children don't stay long knowing the kids want to get back home to play with their new toys.

Milly hands them small parting gifts of homemade peanut brittle and chocolate squares. The little Christmas gift bags, prettily decorated with bows and ribbons, are eye-catching so she's soon enjoined to make up bags for the childless guests to take home as well.

Helena and Christopher Larch arrive and are subjected to intense scrutiny. Tongues were busy wagging over the shocking revelation of him having a previously-unknown daughter. Local opinion is evenly divided over whether the couple's marriage can withstand that discovery.

The leading gossips make friendly overtures drawing the couple into their conversation. Since Helena has known the three older women her whole life she's careful with her responses. Chris was briefed by his mother-in-law about what to expect so he simply smiles with charming deference. Unable to find fault the ladies are forced to settle with saying that *it's too soon to tell.*

When Esther comes into the room arm-in-arm with Amelia all eyes are on the two teenagers. They're especially keen to know all about Amelia, about her late mother, what her future holds, and the poor girl is peppered with probing questions. Samuel can hear an edge developing in Amelia's voice and knowing how short a fuse his own daughter has manages to intervene by calling the girls away to lend a hand in the kitchen.

Once she's out of the room Amelia blows out a relieved breath giving a heartfelt: "Thank you, Mr. Young. I sure wasn't expecting to be asked so many questions—"

"Rapid fire!" Esther adds.

"Yeah, they barely waited for me to answer! You know, my life isn't anything special so why do they want to know all about it?"

"Because they're old and nosy and you're young and new," states Esther sharply.

Samuel gently reprimands her then suggests they each fill up a plate and go hide in Esther's room. The girls agree and he watches with a fond smile as they pile up sweet treats, chattering non-stop.

Back in the sitting-room the crowd has dwindled to half-a-dozen. Both Milly and Nora are surprised to hear Luisa Bautista and Peter Showalty's names paired romantically. It seems one of the remaining couples saw the two of them having dinner in San Luis Obispo and the harpies on the sofa are loudly drawing their own conclusions.

Uncomfortable with the turn the conversation has taken Milly mentions that Dr. Bautista is expected to arrive at any moment. "She's very kindly delivering our poor Bernie back to us after him spending the night at her clinic."

The minute the words leave her mouth she's aware of the Young brothers eyeballing her with chagrined expressions. Puzzled, she turns to Nora who makes a show of rolling her eyes towards the Misses Harrigan and Janice Peart. Milly reacts with a quiet *oh!* belatedly realizing her mistake.

There's no way these women will leave before Luisa arrives and satisfies their curiosity. Just as the realization sinks in the room rings with the sound of anxious barking. Bernie is home and demanding to know what's been going on in his absence.

The puppy rushes into the room and darts from one person to the other, excitedly licking Milly's face before galloping over to Daniel and reaching up to put his paws on Daniel's knees. Delighted that his dog has recovered so completely Daniel reaches down to hold Bernie's head and look into his brown eyes asking *who's a good boy, hmm? who? is it you?* Bernie lets his wildly wagging tail answer for him. Milly grins to see the two of them so happy with each other.

Luisa comes into the room followed by Peter Showalty and knowing looks are exchanged among the older women. Nora is pleasantly intrigued, wishing only the best for her friend. Milly shares the feeling, knowing Peter is a good man and a great catch. Daniel stands to shake hands and thank Luisa for taking such good care of his pet.

"He had a rough go of it, Daniel, so make sure he gets plenty of rest and drinks lots of water over the next few days. He isn't 100 percent yet but he'll get there."

"I'll take him outside for a quick walk," says Daniel.

"Good idea. He'll be happy to mark his territory again," the vet replies with a chuckle.

"I'll say goodnight now ladies, Chris and Peter, because I expect this guy will want to do a full inspection of the property."

Chris bends down to give Bernie a quick scratch on top of his head. The puppy has won him over completely. Samuel suspects that if Amelia wants to ask her father for a dog he'll happily give in once they move into their own place. He decides to suggest it, thinking the care of a shared pet will be a good bonding experience for all three of them.

Daniel leaves and the women turn their attention on the new couple with a laser-sharp focus. Peter has spent a career dealing with hopeful matchmakers so he merely stares back with a smile. After a long silence a tiny frown appears on Luisa's brow as she struggles to understand what's causing the tension in the room. Fortunately her friend provides a distraction.

"Luisa, Milly was telling me about your *Orphan's Holiday Meal* and I'm fascinated. That's a great idea, who thought of it?" Nora enquires.

The three older ladies bite back the questions they were going to ask in order to learn all about this new topic. Hannah joins in with a few comments of her own and that conversation carries them through another half-hour until Jim Cairns arrives to pick up his wife and Samuel asks if he wouldn't mind taking the remaining guests home?

"Not at all, I was just about to offer. The car is already warmed up so it's nice and toasty. I'll bring it up to the kitchen door, that's closest."

The women are left with no good reason to delay or refuse. Hannah escorts them upstairs to use the facilities and get into their coats. Janice Peart came downstairs first and tells Milly she should give her another gift bag to pass on to Miz Tally when she gets back home. The thought of the octogenarian chomping down on peanut brittle brings a smile to Milly's face but she agrees readily and gives Janice a second bag.

After lengthy goodbyes all the guests, with the exception of Luisa and Peter, finally depart. Daniel returns saying *I saw Jim's car full of twittering hens so I knew the coast was clear*, and everyone laughs at his description.

"You know, it really is a strain trying to have a conversation while watching every single word in case it gets twisted or misconstrued."

"Exhausting!" agrees Nora. "They're like cats outside a mouse-hole just waiting to pounce."

"Make up your mind, sweetheart. They can't be hens and cats," Amos teases.

It's Peter who answers on Nora's behalf saying: "I've worked with your wife for several years now Amos, and I wouldn't dare try to win an argument against her."

"Thanks, boss!"

"Oh Peter," groans Amos, "don't encourage her!"

A Dinner Date

"It's really cold out so you better bundle up, Milly," Daniel warns as he walks into the kitchen and whistles for Bernie. Seconds later a whirlwind of floppy ears, scrabbling paws, and wildly wagging tail bursts into the room racing around and barking.

"Who said I was going for a walk? Oh alright, I will, but take him out that way," Milly points back to the boot room, flapping her arms at the overexcited dog and laughing man. "I'll grab my stuff and meet you outside."

Soon the three of them are tramping along on the frost-hardened ground heading towards the escarpment. Their faces are bright with smiles and rosy cheeks in the chilly but invigorating air.

Walking hand-in-hand they follow the delighted pup who speeds ahead then turns, runs back to give them a bark, and goes tearing off again.

"Is he telling us to *hurry up!* or checking that we're still following?"

"Goodness knows what Bernie's thinking, sweetheart. He's just being a dog. It doesn't take much to make him happy."

"Me either, Daniel," Milly replies candidly.

He stops to look down into her face. Tightening the scarf at her neck his voice sounds rough as he tells her to *keep your throat covered up or you'll get sick.* Daniel bends to kiss her and their cool lips quickly warm pressed close together. The coldness of their skin contrasts with the heat of their mouths as they embrace.

They stand entwined, lost in each other and oblivious to the temperature, until Bernie headbutts their legs breaking the spell.

Daniel explains to Milly that *we have to be mindful of his feet since the frozen ground can burn the pads of his paws.*

"I would never have thought of something like that. I mean, I know you can't leave a dog inside a car in the summer, probably not in the winter, either, but I never thought about—oh! I guess his feet can get burned on hot sand just like ours do... can he get sunburn?"

"His thick coat protects his body from a strong sun, same as it does against this cold, but yeah, his nose and the inside of his ears can sunburn. This is Bernie's first experience of winter weather and it's turned into an exceptionally frigid December. He'll acclimate, but we have to keep an eye out for him."

They head back to the farmhouse and go straight to the warm kitchen where Bernie settles with the remains of his rawhide bone and Milly makes hot cocoa. Daniel has stopped in the hall and she can hear him on his phone.

He comes in and sits down to enjoy a couple of shortbread cookies with his hot drink saying: "I called Antonacci's and their special Italian Christmas dinner ends at New Year's. I tried to get us reservations for this Friday but they're booked solid, in fact the only night available is tonight. I booked, because I didn't want to lose the spot, but I can cancel if you'd just rather just stay in. I mean it's been non-stop for days now so..."

"No, tonight sounds great! I'm really interested in trying this traditional meal and honestly Daniel, I just love the holiday season here in The Cove. I'm afraid things are going to feel pretty flat in the new year by comparison."

"Except for the début of the Farm Café and of course the new husband... or did you forget about me already?"

"Oh! Oh I didn't mean married life with you would be boring. Oh no, Daniel I—ah, you're teasing me. Well I'll forgive you since we're finally going out on a real date."

"What do you mean by... oh Milly! you're right. We've never actually gone out, just the two of us. Why not? What's wrong with me?"

She just smiles at him and shrugs her shoulders before saying: "I would love to go on a dinner date with you tonight, Daniel. Italian food will be a nice change from all the sweet stuff we've been eating."

"Yes, I've heard that Italians call non-Italians *mangecakes* meaning *cake eaters* so we'll be having lots of savory flavors. The dinner starts early because there are several courses. They ask everyone to be in their seats by 6:00, so if we leave at 5:30 we'll be there in plenty of time.

Oh, and I'll ask Dad if I can take his car so you don't have to worry about showing up in my old truck—"

"Don't you dare! That *lovely* old truck brought you home safely on Christmas Eve so I will always be happy to ride in it," Milly declares.

Daniel wears a black shirt, dress pants, and shoes then adds a cashmere v-neck in light gray. Milly puts on a lavender dress over black leggings and ankle boots. It's a change from their recent Christmas-themed clothes, and the two enjoy dressing up to mark the occasion. Samuel insists on taking a picture before they leave.

After a few photos Milly brings Samuel, Amos, and Nora into the pantry to point out all the leftovers they can use for their own dinner with instructions to fix a plate, add gravy, and pop it in the microwave on the *reheat* setting.

Once assured *we won't starve* she and Daniel head out for their special night.

Antonacci's Trattoria is well-known in the county as a family-run business providing top-quality Italian dishes. It's not a large restaurant and diners are instantly put at east by the convivial atmosphere redolent with roasted garlic that greets them.

Italo Antonacci is the jovial host beaming goodwill and joy while his wife warmly greets and seats the guests.

He explains: "On Christmas Eve we Italians have a feast of 7 fish dishes so the Christmas Day meal is meat-based.

If any of you have ever attended an Italian wedding you'll be familiar with how we serve a variety of courses. You don't have to finish every bite – although you might as well stab your fork into my heart if you don't," he adds in a rehearsed but entertaining manner. "And in between courses you're welcome to have a dance or visit with another table, but if you have to smoke you gotta do that outside."

Clapping his hands he calls "Mangiamo!" and the servers come through from the kitchen bearing plates of deli meats, cheese, olives, and thick-sliced bread with olive oil for dipping instead of butter.

"If you look at the menu on your table, and you can take it home as a Christmas memento, this first course is called *Antipasto*. Now, I will leave you to enjoy!"

Daniel hands Milly the print-out, knowing she's interested in all things food, and after scanning the list she reads it out loud saying:

"Goodness knows how any of these words are pronounced! But I'll try.

- Antipasto: prosciutto, salami, mortadella, mushrooms, olives, roasted red peppers, and provolone
- Fagioli Soup, made with pasta and beans
- Roast Lamb, with Gorgonzola salad and stuffed artichokes

- Porchetta Roast, seasoned pork loin with Parmesan rice
- Roast Beef, served with bacon-wrapped asparagas
- Dolce: Cannoli with Ricotta filling; Tiramisu cake; Panettone, a sweet bread with candied fruit; Struffoli, fried dough drizzled with honey; and Cantucci which are almond biscotti

Wow! That sure is a lot of food!" Milly finishes with a wide-eyed stare.

"Good thing I'm hungry," agrees Daniel.

As it turns out the meal is served in a leisurely fashion that allows time to digest between courses. Some couples get up to dance but Milly and Daniel are content to sit and watch.

The room has a dark décor with red-brick walls, dark hardwood floors, and burgundy drapes and linens. Each table holds a low centerpiece of fat red candles in painted crystal holders surrounded by silk poinsettias and pine cones, all sprinkled with gold sparkles.

The light from the candles reflects the shine on Milly's lips and the flames dance in her eyes. Daniel is entranced by the romantic, poetic mood she inspires in him.

Signor Antonacci makes the rounds at each table carrying a bottle and pouring complimentary glasses. Tonight's meal is a set price with alcoholic beverages costing extra. Most of the diners are very happy to get a drink for free.

When he arrives at their table both Daniel and Milly place a hand over their unused wine-glasses thanking the host but explaining they don't imbibe.

"You don't drink? Then why the big smiles? Why are you two such a happy couple?"

Playing along Daniel says: "Probably because we got engaged last week."

Dramatically throwing up his hands Italo Antonacci shouts to his wife: "Antonia, quickly! We celebrate with that sparkling champagne," and turning to the young couple explains *it's non-alcoholic, but just as bubbly!*

Mrs. Antonacci comes out a minute or so later carrying two full champagne flutes on a tray and her husband encourages a round of applause from the other patrons. The staff call out *congratulazione! bravo!* and *ben fatto!*

Milly's huge smile has her dimples on full display and she's delighted to see Daniel at a loss for words. They clink their glasses in a silent toast to each other then happily take a deep drink.

The date is a great success. The easygoing, unhurried service of an extravagant and delicious meal surrounded by warm camaraderie makes it a memorable experience.

"You're going to be hard-pressed to top this date, Daniel," Milly says, smirking at him.

"Next time we go out for meal we'll be married so it won't be a date," he replies.

"No, I've heard of married people having *date nights.*"

"Yeah, that's something for people who need to schedule their time together on a calendar. You and I will live and work together so there's no chance of us drifting apart."

"We could still have date nights for just the two of us, after the children come along."

Daniel quirks up one eyebrow and with a wry expression huffs: "We could... but if I know you as well as I think I do you'll want to make them family events. You'll probably make me go bowling."

With a gasp of delight Milly states: "I've never been bowling! Can you bowl? I'd love to try it."

"So let's see: I've taught you how to line-dance; we're training the dog, we have swimming lessons coming up this summer, and now I have to teach you to bowl?"

Milly nods vigorously. Pretending to be put upon Daniel heaves a heavy sigh but does so with a smile.

Milly gurgles a laugh agreeing that Daniel does know her so well. "I've always yearned – how's that for an expressive word? *Yearned,* to be part of a family and to have a family of my own.

I know my parents loved me but I only got proof of that recently. Before then, well, I hoped they loved me as parents are supposed to but in truth for almost all of my life I felt abandoned and alone. And—" she breaks off and glances down.

Gently, Daniel says: "Tell me, Milly."

Still keeping her eyes on her plate he can see she takes a deep breath before lifting her head to face him. Wearing a tremulous smile she says: "I will, but not here. This place is purely for pleasure and fun."

Daniel is tempted to press but agrees not to pursue the question now, though he silently resolves to have his answers before the night is over.

By the time the desserts, the *dolce,* are delivered the sound level is high with conversations stretching across the room from table to table. It's a happy, festive crowd of well-fed people celebrating over good food and the holiday season.

A couple explaining *we have a babysitter to get home to* stand up to leave. Milly and Daniel follow soon after having drunk their espresso and politely declined a liqueur.

They sincerely praise the meal, the ambience, and the wonderful occasion promising to be back in the new year to sample the trattoria's famous seafood platter.

Daniel takes hold of Milly's arm and walks her to the passenger side of Samuel's car, which he decided to take after all, and opening the door gets her inside and secures her seat-belt.

Arriving home they discover the family have all turned in for an early night. It's only just after 10:00 but the past few days have been busy. Wrapping themselves up with quilts Daniel again leads Milly outside to sit on the porch swing.

Bernie is allowed to wander around the veranda but he soon returns to lie down near his favorite humans. Of course he makes a point of sighing heavily in that way dogs do to show their displeasure at being left behind.

The cold night is clear enough to showcase a sky full of stars and the sight adds a magical touch to an already perfect evening. Milly snuggles against Daniel's chest and he wraps both arms around her.

They sit silently, their breathing slow and synchronized, enjoying each other's company. Daniel is relieved when Milly continues her earlier conversation without prompting.

"When I said I grew up feeling lonely it wasn't about being unwanted because Sunshine always made her feel welcome, never a burden, but she didn't love me. She was proud of me and said so, just as she said she enjoyed my company, but she never pretended to feel love. Since I knew no one loved me I just ended up accepting that I'm unlovable—"

Daniel's arms tighten around her as he begins: "Oh sweetheart—"

But Milly stops him saying: "No, please let me finish. Let me say this out loud once and then I never have to say it again."

She pauses a moment then accepting his silent agreement continues: "Just because I'd never known love didn't mean I wasn't hopeful for a future with a family of my own I just... I just didn't have very high expectations. I don't know what I imagined but it never came close to what I actually found.

Daniel, living here on the Young's Family Fruit Farm, working in the shop, and getting to know all of you, has been the happiest time of my life. I can't tell you how full my heart is—" her words catch in her throat and she chokes out a sob.

"Oh Milly, Milly, my darling girl," he murmurs kissing the top of her head, the side of her face, finally taking hold of her chin and turning it to find her mouth. Daniel expresses his feelings in a deep, passionate kiss feeding her his air and inhaling her sweet taste. A taste with a touch of salt that makes him realize she's crying.

Pulling back to study her he's reassured to see a shaky smile. He feels stifled, like they're in a bubble of too much emotion, so he breaks the mood demanding to know:

"Milly why don't you taste like garlic? We've just eaten a ton of it."

She giggles, suddenly feeling light and merry, as she explains: "It's because you ate garlic, too. We can't smell or taste it on each other, it's like a taste-bud overload or something."

After some quiet chuckles Daniel tentatively returns to Milly's remarks. "I keep learning more and more about you. I mean, having you in the

191

farmhouse has felt right from Day One. You just fit, like you were exactly where you were supposed to be."

"It's funny you say that because I knew I never fit in at the commune. I was actually two generations younger than the people who raised me so there was always this huge gap in our knowledge and experiences. Yet from the very first morning waking up in my bedroom here I felt like I'd found my home."

"You did. You found it in our family when you settled into my heart. You know I think that's partly why it took me so long to propose. I figured you just knew that we were meant to be – and would be – together."

"That's all true, but... a girl likes to be romanced a bit," she states, looking up through her lashes at him.

Time is suspended as Daniel returns her look feeling a surge of heat through his blood. He abruptly stands and gruffly says: "It's getting late, we better go in."

Milly is disconcerted until she feels his hand at her back, gently guiding her inside. He strokes her hair back from her face and tenderly kisses her cheek.

"Goodnight, sweetheart. Thank you for going out with me tonight, it was great."

"Thank you Daniel for taking me to dinner. I had a wonderful time."

"You go ahead up to bed while I lock up and get Bernie settled. Sweet dreams, Milly. Only four more sleeps until our wedding day."

Car Shopping with Daniel

Daniel has come to the Farm Shop to assist Milly, or at least to keep her company. As expected, business dropped off quite a bit after Christmas. Folks are still enjoying the chocolate and candy gifts that were left under the tree, and eating up the remnants of this year's Christmas baking.

Come the new year these same people will resolve to lose a few pounds so the sweet treats Milly bakes won't be in heavy demand until Valentine's. She's hoping the little café will draw in customers. In the meantime she's quite happy to enjoy the slower pace and visit with her fiancé.

"So although I really love the Miata I saw at the Mazda dealership I'm having second thoughts about it."

"Why? is it the price? because you know I can help out–" Daniel offers. He still isn't completely comfortable with Milly's new-found wealth.

"Aw that's sweet Daniel but no, it's not the cost, well yes it is expensive even after Nora's dickering with that salesman," she breaks off to chuckle saying: "You wouldn't believe the dramatics! But no, I was thinking that a two-seater is really a selfish car, I mean where would Bernie sit?"

Daniel smiles at comment and her earnest look before asking what car she has in mind now.

She perks up saying: "A little Honda Civic. They're so cute! but they still have plenty of room inside."

"Well the Civic is certainly a more practical choice–" he begins but she cuts him off.

"Oh Daniel, sometimes I just get sick and tired of always being practical!"

He's surprised at the note of despair in her voice and pulls her into his arms for a cuddle. "Milly, there's nothing dull or boring about you and never will be no matter how pragmatic or phlegmatic you get."

"Ugh! that sounds horrible!"

"Well it isn't. It not only means that you're calm, cool, and collected but also that you're serene and tranquil and that's exactly the type of woman this man wants to come home to at the end of the day."

She lifts her eyes, her expression cautiously hopeful, to meet his gaze saying: "Oh! really?"

He answers in a firm voice: "Yes, really. Really and truly."

"Thank you for saying that, Daniel. It's reassuring."

"Good and besides, if you had of gotten that two-door car you'd have paid way more for insurance, they add a premium when it's a sports-model."

Milly giggles at her handsome Daniel being so sensible.

"Hey, Amos said he finished up his to-do list this morning and was going to spend the afternoon hanging out with Nora since she's off work so I'm gonna call him to come and relieve us. The shop's only open for another two hours anyhow so they can cover it while you and I go to the Honda dealership."

"Oh can we? Daniel that sounds wonderful! but... do you think you can haggle as well as Nora? She was really effective using her *powers of female persuasion*," Milly teases.

"Well... if the salesperson is female then sure, I fancy my chances." He smirks as Milly gives his arm a smack, pretending to be jealous.

Although she'd never admit it deep down she does wonder what Daniel sees in her. Milly knows she is pretty in a wholesome girl-next-door way, and she tries her best to be a nice person, but knows she's not exciting or sexy or worldly. Even though it's obvious Daniel likes his quiet life she can't help but worry *what if he gets bored with me?*

If Daniel could know Milly's thoughts he'd be amazed and annoyed at what he'd call *her silly thinking.* He envisions a long and happy married life with them loving each other easily and comfortably.

He considers Milly's lack of ego and drama a godsend, and her placid nature is a huge part of her attraction. Unfortunately Daniel doesn't put that into the words she needs to hear for reassurance, but the quick hug and squeeze he gives her certainly helps.

He calls up Amos and in no time at all his brother and sister-in-law arrive to take over the Farm Shop duties.

Despite gray clouds on this drab day Milly and Daniel are cheerful. Milly chatters throughout the drive and Daniel enjoys the enthusiasm he hears in her pleasantly modulated voice. She sings along to the chorus of a song playing on the radio and he surprises them both by joining in. Their voices blend in perfect harmony.

The Honda dealership has a huge selection of used and new vehicles, everything from compact cars to full-size SUVs. Milly is determined to get a brand-new car and carefully avoids looking at the marked-down prices scrawled on the windshields screaming *SALE!* and *DEALS!*

Daniel patiently follows behind as she's escorted from car to car by a salesman expounding on each one's features. When he turns to Daniel to discuss under the hood specs Daniel defers to Milly explaining *it's entirely my fiancée's decision.* Milly reaches to hold his hand and he gives hers a comforting squeeze.

After checking out every vehicle in the showroom she narrows it down between two models and then discusses colors. Finally she makes her choice on the condition it's available to drive away today. The salesman agrees, and leads them to an office to deal with paperwork.

As a long pre-printed order form is produced and the man begins talking about delivery and distribution fees, dealership service packages, taxes and EPA fees and carbon capture schemes, Daniel gives him a hard look. He doesn't have to say a word but Milly can feel the weight of his staring presence as can the salesman who strokes out a number of items from the price list offering *to take care of these for her.*

Finally a final dollar amount is presented. At this point another employee, an older man, comes in and the salesman introduces him as *our Finance guru.* Smiling broadly the man reaches to shake hands but everyone pulls back remembering the *new normal* of contact-free greetings post-Covid. Picking up the finalized sales sheet he quickly scans it and then explains what terms he can offer for a payment plan.

Milly listens carefully as he runs through the costs for 60-, 72-, and even 84-month contracts if necessary to make the financing affordable.

"Thank you, that's very clear. Now, what kind of a discount will you offer for cash?"

Daniel rubs his nose so he can cover the smile on his mouth at Milly's young voice politely but firmly making the request. Her demeanor hasn't changed and she's disconcerted the men.

"Cash? for the whole price?" exclaims the salesman.

The Finance Manager states: "Our terms are very competitive but if your bank if offering a better deal well... we could probably match it."

"Oh! no, I'm not borrowing. I have the cash now," she replies adding shyly: "I've been saving up for a long time."

The two employees exchange a look and it's obvious the salesman wants to close the deal. "Well, it's an unusual request, we don't have a cash discount because almost no one pays cash for a new car..." his voice trails off, but Daniel speaks up asking *do you offer a senior's discount?*

"We do!" The older man grasps at the suggestion and assures them the 5% savings provided to seniors can be applied to their cash purchase as well.

Beaming, Milly says: "That's great, thank you! Where do I sign? and what name should I put on the check?"

After another hour of paperwork to transfer ownership, sign Milly on to the Young's insurance policy, and register the license plate they all head over to the car. A worker in overalls is removing the paper coverings off the floor-mats and the protective plastic that's wrapped around the mirrors before moving the car outside.

The salesman congratulates Milly on her purchase and says he'll walk her out to the lot where she can take possession. Once she's given the key and seated inside they all comment on that *new car smell*. Milly is grinning so widely she feels like her face will split open.

"You get started, sweetheart, and I'll be following right behind you," promises Daniel. Milly nods and drives towards the road.

The men watch closely, noticing she carefully holds the steering wheel in the ten to two position. When they spy her giving a little shimmy of a happy dance, they chuckle and congratulate Daniel on his forthcoming marriage.

Farm Shop Stand-ins

Amos is happy to take a turn manning the Farm Shop since he has Nora to keep him company. It's such a dreary, chilly day they don't expect many – if any – customers so they get themselves comfortable to chat until three o'clock. Legs stretched out they sit side-by-side on a couple of chairs.

"I'm glad Daniel is taking Milly car-shopping. The way he acted the first time she mentioned getting a car was a total buzzkill."

"Oh I know, and he hurt her feelings, too," Nora agrees, scowling at the memory. "You know, that was only a week ago but it seems much longer, doesn't it?"

"Yeah but it's been a very busy week, I mean the engagement then all the run-up to Christmas and Bernie getting sick–"

"Oh and Miz Tally getting sick and all the gossip and Milly standing up to that Janice Peart," interrupts Nora, sitting up.

"Yeah I heard that was epic! and the good news of Miz Tally recovering. Plus our very busy Open House on Boxing Day."

"Oh that reminds me. Amos, have you been holding out on me?" Nora's tone is teasing but she gives her husband a penetrating look. He knows he better fess up to whatever she's found out. Unfortunately he has no idea what she's talking about.

"What do you mean?"

"I mean Peter Showalty, your best friend, seeing Luisa? Is that really a thing or is it just the old biddies gossiping?"

It's obvious from his expression that he's considering the idea for the first time and hasn't been keeping secrets from her.

"Oh that. Um, yeah... he did say something but I don't remember..." he trails off.

"Huh! Not good enough, buster. Spill the tea," she demands.

"Well I really don't remember, but, uh... he was talking about her a lot... and um... about how funny she is, she does have a wicked sense of humor, and how easy she is to talk to. That's it yeah, that's what he said about her."

"But are they dating?"

"Oh, I don't know. Lemme think... well they did have a dinner out, but I don't know if it was a date–"

"That's what we heard, that they were spotted having dinner in SLO, just the two of them. Sounds like a date to me," Nora decides. She's swung her legs around and is facing Amos, her body language clearly showing her interest in the subject.

"Well she's your best friend so you should know as much as I do – if not more!"

Making an exasperated noise Nora complains: "Oh you know what Luisa's like, she doesn't talk about herself at all."

Crowding into her personal space Amos teases: "Or maybe you never give her a chance to talk?"

Laughing she shoves him in the chest but Amos is a big bulky man and he doesn't budge. Since their faces are only inches apart he takes advantage and gives his wife a kiss. Nora responds with enthusiasm and it's a few minutes before they break apart.

"We're lucky that Janice Peart didn't come in to interrupt us shouting "*Aha! caught you!*"

"Yeah, Milly did mention the woman tends to drop in close to quitting time and it's almost 3:00 now."

"Hey, aren't Thursdays the day Stephen sends someone here to pick up Milly's donations?"

"You're right. He asked and Milly offered right away, but surely they aren't having any functions on during Christmas week?"

"Hmm, probably not. Which would explain why Milly never said anything to us."

"Except she was pretty excited about Daniel volunteering to take her car-shopping so maybe she forgot?"

"I'll go check out back and see if there's anything prepared."

Amos opens the door into the short hallway and a moment later calls out from the storeroom *found it!* Nora gets up to hold the door open while her husband comes through carrying two large cellophane-wrapped cardboard trays.

They can see the contents through the film and one tray is cupcakes with brightly colored icing and heavily sprinkled donuts, while the other is butter tarts and date squares sitting on Christmas patterned doilies.

"I guess she didn't need to label which is which," chuckles Amos.

Looking over the attractive packages Nora whines: "Awww, now I'm getting hungry!"

"We could sneak out a couple of treats and just move the other stuff around to cover up the gap?" Amos poses it as a question and Nora is considering her answer when the lights of a car shine across the front of the shop.

At this time of year the sky has already darkened by mid-afternoon. They hear a door slam and heavy footsteps hurrying up the path. It's Stephen Smithson full of apologies for running late today.

"Actually you just saved us from temptation," quips Nora with a smile.

"Well yes that kind of is my job... what exactly were you two fighting against?" Stephen asks jovially. The cold air has put color in his cheeks and his eyes twinkle with his usual good humor.

With a guilty look Nora confesses: "Pilfering a couple of Milly's treats from these boxes, they all look so good!"

Leaning over to get a closer look Stephen agrees Milly's donations are mouthwatering. "My sweet tooth is my secret vice," he admits. "But I'm afraid if I start I won't stop so I think it's best if I just whisk these delicious temptations out of the way."

The three of them agree that's the smart thing to do and Amos says: "I'll carry the trays, Rev, while you get the door and open the car."

The men head out the front and Nora fetches the coats so she and Amos can go out the back way to walk home. She's feeling virtuous for not stealing a dessert and consoles herself by remembering the many tins of baked treats waiting in the farmhouse.

Hearing the bell over the front door tinkle when Amos comes back in Nora calls out *I've got our coats* and her husband locks the door.

When he joins her he's got a rueful look as he says: "I forgot that I promised Hannah I would pick up Jim's medication from Michaelson's pharmacy. I'll walk you home and grab the car to nip down there. Joseph will have it ready and waiting so I won't be gone long."

"No problem, I wanted to pick up some antihistamine from there anyhow. I don't know if it's me eating too much sugar lately, or being around all the woolens, but I've been breaking out in little patches of hives and the itching drives me crazy."

Dropping his voice to a gravelly whisper Amos coos: "Poor baby... let me rub calomine lotion all over you."

"I think the oral medication will do the trick, but thanks!" she retorts sarcastically.

Amos just laughs saying: "I'll just leave that offer on the table for you..."

Cindy the Civic

Daniel is in his truck following Milly proudly driving her brand-new Honda Civic hatchback. The exterior shade of blue matches her eyes and the cream-colored interior has a luxe look. She's going a little under the speed limit since the salesman told her to *go slow to break the engine in for about the first 500 miles.*

Pulling into the kitchen yard Milly beeps her horn until Hannah comes to see *who's making all that noise?* She's got Bernie with her and he's excited to greet Milly and sniff all all over the new car.

"Don't you dare pee on it," she warns the dog, pushing him off so his claws don't scratch the paint.

"Well well, so you did get yourself a car after all," smiles Hannah, giving the compact vehicle a satisfactory nod.

"Isn't she gorgeous?"

"She?"

"Yes! meet *Cindy the Civic.* My very first car, my Christmas present to myself, and I plan to drive her for years and years."

Now Samuel and Esther come out and compliment Milly on her purchase. Esther calls the car *cute* and jumping in the passenger seat stretches out saying: "And look, there's tons of room. I love the colors, Milly."

Daniel has parked his truck and walked around to join them. The car in the kitchen yard makes him think about the first time he ever saw Milly. He marvels to think that was only... five months ago? no, just four-and-a-half. Five months ago he didn't even know Milly Clarke existed... impossible to believe now!

He remembers that although he hadn't heard a car he assumed she drove and looked out the door to see where she'd parked her vehicle. Discovering she'd taken a taxi and the driver had left her to walk all the way up the long driveway carrying a big suitcase – in the rain, too – he'd been suddenly, irrationally angry.

He took it out on Milly by giving her the cold shoulder and being rude. *At least I got that driver, lazy Gerry, squared away*, he recalls with grim satisfaction.

He'd been surprised to learn Milly didn't even own a car, she never had. But she'd already started saving up to buy something used.

The windfall from her late parents' estate, fortunately discovered before defaulting unclaimed back to the State, means she can afford this new car and plenty of other things as well.

Daniel determinedly tamps down the little niggle of affronted pride telling himself that *Milly isn't the type to flaunt or fritter away her money. Besides, nowadays it's common for couples to each have their own nest egg when come together. He knows Nora has savings, she's been working for a number of years, and Amos is happy that she has something of her own.*

Daniel loves observing Milly's excitement as she demonstrates the car's many features, spouting a jumble of facts and figures, and highlighting the sensing technology that earned Honda an excellent safety rating.

"It's the biggest purchase I've ever made, and the most expensive thing – by far – that I've ever bought for myself."

Daniel smiles thinking *she's beside herself with the joy of owning her very own car. Now I feel bad for being so dismissive about it. After all, what do I know about buying a brand-new car? I drive a pick-up truck that's older than Milly!*

Nora and Amos had gone into The Cove to pick up a few things after closing up the Farm Shop and now join everyone in the kitchen yard. They're both suitably impressed with Milly's new car and Nora declares that *Cindy* is a better choice than the Miata.

Milly rhapsodizes about the freedom it gives her, the thrill of her purchasing power, and the pride of ownership, and Nora is completely attuned to that mind-set.

Even Esther, who hasn't yet taken her written driver's test although she's been eligible for more than a year, is feeling the excitement.

Amos now asks if the dealership got Milly all sorted with her paperwork.

"Yes, they provided the licence plate and vehicle registration. Daniel called his insurance agent to set up an account for me, and my bank sent a FAX confirming my check is good. Oh! I need to update my driver's license with my new address in Sweet Berry Cove."

"And your new name after we get married," puts in Daniel.

Grinning Milly confirms: "That's right! I'll do both at the same time."

Amos shakes his head explaining the address change has to be made within six months so she can't wait much longer, and certainly not until next Fall or Winter.

Careful not to meet Daniel's eye Milly's face is serious as she agrees that *no, she won't wait that long.*

The Village Party

The adults of the Young household are walking into town and they're amused at Bernie dragging behind, sulky at being put on a leash.

Milly feels sorry for him but Daniel is getting annoyed. He stops and confronts his pup commanding heel! and the sullen Saint Bernard obeys but... Nora bursts out laughing claiming *Bernie's got the face of a teenager today!* They all laugh at that and as if understanding he's the butt of the joke the dog turns his head away from them.

"Speaking of teenagers, where is little sis?"

"Son you're not so old you can't remember how mortifying it is to hang out with your family in public, right?" asks Samuel with a chuckle.

"Oooh great! I can't wait to embarrass her in front of her friends..."

"You'll do no such thing, husband," Nora chides. "Maybe you were thick-skinned as a teen but Esther isn't so you're going to leave her alone."

"Thick-headed, for sure," quips Daniel and Amos elbows him.

"Stop bickering boys, I'm looking forward to this party," states their father.

"It's just one celebration after another!" enthuses an excited Milly. She's full of questions about tonight's event.

"Yes, it's tradition in The Cove that the Saturday before New Year's Eve is always reserved for the village party, a get-together with a pot-luck supper that's really just snack foods, and fireworks."

"Fireworks! And line-dancing?"

Amos explains: "No, because there's a square-dancing contest which is always entertaining to watch."

"Is it in the school auditorium again?"

"No, no, this party is more informal. It's not a commercial event, none of the stores will be open for trade, but each will have a goodies table set up in front. The villagers walk up and down Main Street wandering in and out, sampling the treats.

It's more of a street fair rather than a formal party and we don't advertise or invite tourists," Samuel elaborates.

"I'm glad we've got warmer temperatures for a few days but even so, being outdoors still means we had to get all bundled up."

"Not us square-dancers. We'll shuck our coats as soon as we begin the routines. We get a real workout and that keeps us warm."

"You're a square-dancer, Samuel?"

"I am indeed. I've been partnering Martha Hannaford for years and we've even won a ribbon or two."

"Don't be modest, Dad," puts in Daniel. "You two always come in first or second every time."

"Really? I can't wait to see you perform. Oh! I love Christmas at Sweet Berry Cove," Milly exclaims. She catches Daniel's eye and the two share a smile over the secret that tomorrow will be their wedding day.

As a rule Sweet Berry Cove rolls up the sidewalk early so Milly has never been in the village after dark before. There are no street lights so normally it would be pitch black, but tonight every storefront is decorated with Christmas lights and the effect is magical.

It's crowded enough that it looks like every single inhabitant of The Cove is out mingling on Main Street. Unfortunately the first person the Youngs' encounter is Janice Peart.

The dressing-down Milly gave the old gossip is now part of village lore but both women choose to pretend it never happened and Milly is the first to call out a cheerful "Good Evening, Janice!" She no longer calls the older woman *Mrs. Peart*.

"It is, I always enjoy the village party. I was that vexed when it seemed we'd have to cancel it when we had that Covid scare, but I'm happy to say most of us still turned out and nobody got sick."

Samuel diplomatically compliments Janice on her outfit. Although her square-dance dress is the traditional style of gingham and lace with a starched petticoat the colors are anything but! Shocking pink and canary yellow ensure Janice's costume will draw every eye. Unfortunately the bright color combination doesn't suit her complexion or her age.

"Why Samuel Young you've certainly seen this dress before, I wear it every year!" Milly and Nora exchange a horrified glance at seeing Janice flirt, but Samuel is his usual gallant self.

He extends an arm to Janice who happily links hers with his. Walking ahead of the younger generation she definitely sashays in her starched petticoats. Everyone is smiling, but for different reasons.

"Tally got home this afternoon. I did my best to talk her into coming tonight but she said the long car trip was tiring so she's just going to rest. She wants to be at her best for your New Year's Eve party tomorrow. We're all looking forward to it."

Conversation becomes difficult once they arrive in the midst of the noisy crowd. Everyone is in a celebratory mood and there's praise for all the edible treats being offered.

Milly is fascinated, tasting all of the different flavor combinations, and declaring each one *my new favorite!* Along with the usual hot roasted chestnuts and toffee-coated apples there are also chocolate-dipped potato chips, peanut-butter popcorn balls, deep-fried candy bars... a seemingly endless list of delicious snack foods.

Despite meandering slowly, pausing to have a bite and stopping to have a chat, it doesn't take long to complete the round of shops. The crowd gathers around a makeshift dance-floor overlooked by a dais holding the musicians with their fiddles, banjo, and an accordion. In the middle stands the caller, the man who directs the dancers with cues and prompts, and Milly is surprised to see it's Jim Cairns, Hannah's husband.

Turning to Daniel she says: "I knows Jim is practically a professional line-dancer but I had no idea he had this skill as well. I suppose it makes sense..." She breaks off when the music blares and Jim's voice welcomes the dancers to the floor and begins rapidly calling the steps in a blur of *circle left, Do Si Do, greet your partner, right grand, promenade home...*

The dancers are a swirl of color as they spin in complicated patterns. The toe-tapping music has the audience clapping along and shouting encouragement to favorites. Samuel forbade his sons to do so but Nora startles them all with a piercing two-fingered whistle. The dance competition is a wonderful spectacle and everyone is enjoying themselves.

Helena and Chris Larch have made their way over to stand with the Young's and lend support to their dancing parents. "Have you seen the girls?" asks Helena.

Nora nods across the square to a huddle of teenagers. Chuckling she says: "They're standing over there, as far away from us as they can possibly get!"

"Oh bless 'em, so they are."

Nora's chuckle turns to laughter at Helena's very southern insult. The two women are barely acquainted but get along very well each time they meet.

After four dances the top three winners are declared. Samuel and Martha have won second, Janice and Jay Somers are third, and a considerably older couple who Milly doesn't know won first place.

The dancers graciously accept congratulations although there is an awkward moment when Kay Somers loudly complains that her brother should have partnered her instead of *the clumsy oaf I was saddled with*. Janice smirks and flutters her green ribbon.

The first boom of the fireworks show effectively ends any conversation as all eyes lift skywards to *ooh* and *ahh* over the noisy, colorful displays. Bernie gives a couple of barks in response to the bangs but then settles with his head tilted up looking interested. A few frightened dogs howl and their owners take them away.

Daniel starts to say something to Milly but pauses when he catches sight of her upturned face, full of wonder and delight. The firework's brilliant colors play across her rapt features, and when she glances back at him her eyes reflect the bright shine. A pleasurable surge of warmth infuses him and he reaches his arm around her shoulders to pull her close.

Daniel can't resist kissing Milly, and does so without caring who is watching or what they might think. He's overwhelmed by happiness and that emotion makes this kiss mean more than any other has before.

He murmurs *tomorrow* against her lips and Milly's mouth softens in surrender as she echoes *yes, tomorrow, my love.*

Nora and Amos ask them to a get-together they're going on to with friends but Milly and Daniel have a wordless communication with their eyes and decline the invitation. They're contentedly enjoying each other's company and the pyrotechnic display.

A Quiet Wedding

"Oh don't you look pretty this morning, Milly," exclaims Nora seating herself at the table for breakfast. "You're putting us to shame! We didn't want to wake up this morning and I'm sure it shows."

Amos nods in agreement adding: "We'd skip Church today except that won't look good with us hosting the New Year's Eve party tonight."

Samuel chuckles asking: "Are you afraid people will think the party's canceled? or you just don't want Stephen to get on your case?"

"Both, I guess," Amos agrees sheepishly.

"There isn't much left to do to get ready for tonight's party so I'm sure you can have a lie-down this afternoon," comments Samuel. Turning to look at Milly he says: "I do agree with Nora, my dear. You look exceptionally pretty in that dress, I don't recall seeing it before?"

Blushing at the compliment Milly is about to answer when Daniel comes in, also dressed up more than usual. Milly thinks *he's devastatingly handsome* and she loses all track of the conversation.

Daniel intently stares right back at her and Nora archly remarks: "Look at you two giving each other *heart eyes*."

"Heart eyes!" exclaims Samuel, "What a perfection expression."

"Yeah, yeah," grumbles Amos. "Hurry up and eat your breakfast Daniel, and let's get going."

His brother cocks an eyebrow at him and Esther teases that *Amos is a grouchy, grumpy sleepyhead* and everyone laughs at that description, even Amos himself.

"Nora, why did we stay so late at Peter's last night?"

Counting off the reasons on her fingers Nora explains: "One, it was a Saturday night; two, the week between Christmas and New Year's is non-stop celebrating; and three, we wanted to continue the fun we had with Peter and Luisa at the village party. There was plenty of food, that six-pack of wine coolers, and the conversation was great so we ended up staying longer than we meant to."

Groaning her husband concedes she's right.

"You drank wine?" Milly asks in a shocked voice.

Nora smiles at her facial expression stating that yes, they do have the occasional drink. "But only privately, we respect The Cove's dry policy."

"But is it legal?"

Despite his lethargy Amos explains that while no place in Sweet Berry Cove is licensed to sell alcohol there's no reason folks can't enjoy a drink in their own homes if they choose.

"Remember that one time we traveled up the coast to the Napa Valley for a long weekend?" asks Nora. "It was fun visiting the wineries for sample tastings, but it's like eating cotton candy: something you'll do at a fair but would never bother with at home."

"We never have alcohol here at the farmhouse, Milly, but when you two move into your own place, even though it's on Young property you'll be able to do what you like," says Samuel.

"I have no interest in that. Sunshine was very clear on the dangers of drink. I don't expect to ever taste alcohol," she avers. "Daniel have you... do you drink?"

"I tried it at a frat party in college but I was sick to my stomach all night and hungover all morning. I swore off it then and have never felt the urge to revisit that decision," he confesses.

"Well I don't mind what anyone else does, that's their business, but I'm glad you don't," Milly admits.

Sunday breakfasts are light by necessity because it always seems to be a rush to get them all off to church on time. Today is no exception. While they hurry around getting ready Samuel says: "I'll warm up your SUV Amos, we'll need the room."

"Are you coming to church today, Dad?"

"Yes, Stephen asked me specifically because he said there's a surprise planned."

Nora and Esther stop putting on their coats to demand *what surprise?* Daniel looks panicky but Milly smoothly states: "I'm going to sing *Amazing Grace* at the service."

"Really? How wonderful! Amos, do you remember Milly singing *Somewhere Over The Rainbow* just before we went to the Halloween Party?"

"I do. You have a marvelous voice Milly, and a solo from you will be a treat to listen to."

"Thank you. I was going to sing *Ave Maria* but the Reverend said there would be objections to that song. I don't know why... maybe because it's in Latin?"

Chuckling, Samuel corrects her: "No Milly, the objection would be because it's considered a Catholic hymn celebrating the Virgin Mary."

"Oh! I see, I guess... it's a shame though because it's a beautiful song even if you don't know what the words mean."

"That's why you're wearing make-up and that lacy white dress!" exclaims Esther, "It's because you're getting up in front of the whole village to sing."

Milly smiles and Daniel says: "Okay family, let's go. Milly can't be late for her debut." As Milly walks past him to go outside Daniel snags her arm and pulling her close whispers: "You're just full of surprises, aren't you?"

"I hope I can always find ways to surprise you, Daniel," she replies giving him a close-mouthed smile that pops one dimple out.

"Come ON," Amos calls out impatiently.

They normally walk to Sunday service at the Calvary Church but today is particularly cold and they're already running late. It's a quick trip by car so the family manage to arrive on time. There's a good turnout and the congregants are happy to crowd together to share the warmth of each other's winter coats.

Reverend Stephenson preaches about the opportunities the new year brings. He references *Corinthians: Therefore, if anyone is in Christ, he is a new creation. The old has passed away; behold, the new has come* and at the conclusion of his sermon he gesture for Milly to come up.

Milly doesn't feel at all nervous about singing in the church so she's calm and composed as she joins the Reverend. She's relieved to see that today's organist is Joanie Robson, the school secretary. Mrs. Robson shares the rotation with Kay Somers and Myrna Harrigan and those two ladies are inclined to add their own flourishes and other personal touches when playing.

The packed room listens to Milly sing without a single cough, baby's cry, or shuffling of feet. Her beautiful voice honors the emotion of the hymn, poignantly conveying its message of hope and redemption. When she finishes the congregation breaks into spontaneous applause, even though they're in church.

The Reverend doesn't admonish them, instead he beams at Milly thanking her for her *lovely, stirring performance.*

Daniel possesses a good singing voice himself and recognizes Milly's talent. Listening to the pure, clear notes he's entranced by his beautiful fiancée. In her lacy dress, with her dark hair curled and styled, and her eyes enhanced with mascara, Milly is simply stunning and Daniel admires her poise and grace.

Most of the churchgoers loiter after the service, happily chit-chatting with each other. Amos is in a hurry to get back home and hustles through the crowd as discreetly as possible, towing Nora along with him.

Esther is going on to a friend's place and Samuel is staying for lunch with Stephen. Turning impatiently Amos catches Daniel's eye and jerks his head in a *let's go* gesture.

"You go ahead," calls Daniel. "Milly and I are meeting with the Rev to find out what the requirements are now that we're engaged. We'll walk back afterwards." Amos salutes him in reply.

Milly looks up at Daniel and says: "He's going to be mad at you, isn't he?"

Smirking, Daniel nods and says: "Oh yeah."

After waving goodbye to the last parishioner Stephen closes the oversized door. He gives one loud clap of his hands as he turns with a big smile on his face to ask: "Are we ready?"

Taking Milly's hand Daniel tells Samuel: "Dad, Milly and I are getting married today – now, actually – and we'd be honored to have you share this moment with us and be our witness."

Samuel gapes, speechless, but then a huge grin spreads across his face and his eyes shine bright with happiness. "This is such a surprise! but a wonderful one," he hastens to add. "I'm completely taken aback, I had no idea... Stephen you kept this a secret from me! but oh, I'm just delighted!"

Milly and Daniel decided not to write their own vows. The words Reverend Smithson speaks are traditional and weighty, but heartfelt. Since Stephen is a close friend to both of them the quick ceremony is relaxed and comfortable.

Milly's eyes are brimming but she blinks the tears away when she answers the Reverend's question: "Melisandre Elizabeth Clarke do you take Daniel Axel Young to be your lawfully wedded husband?" with a firm *I do.*

Daniel's voice turns husky as he pledges his eternal love *till death do us part.*

When he slips the wedding band on her ring finger she grips his hands tightly, and when Stephen declares *you may now kiss the bride* Daniel's lips are gentle but determined in his claiming of her mouth.

Samuel draws both of them into his embrace excitedly saying: "Isn't it perfect that we're having a party tonight? What a great way to celebrate! What a perfect way to start off a new year! Oh Stephen I'm going to have to take a rain check for lunch, I have to go home and tell the family and we'll need to get a photographer for tonight oh! and put an announcement in the paper, and–"

Interrupting his father Daniel says "Slow down! We'll announce it to the family when we're all back home this afternoon, and to the neighbors at the party tonight."

"You stay and enjoy your lunch with Stephen while my husband walks me home," adds Milly cheerfully.

"Husband..." Daniel exhales quietly. His eyes meet Milly's and his father, their minister, even the Calvary Church cease to exist for the lovestruck newlyweds.

Without saying thank you or goodbye they head down the aisle and out the door, pausing only long enough to slip back into the winter coats they'd discarded in their pew.

Stephen looks at his good friend and says "Congratulations, Samuel. You've gained another daughter."

"Hallelujah!" the older man replies.

Ringing in the New Year

The farmhouse is quiet when they return with closed bedroom doors signifying the residents are napping. The TV isn't on, no radios are playing, and even Esther's room is silent with none of the usual pop music blaring. It feels strange, making Daniel and Milly very aware of each other, and careful not to disturb anyone with noise.

Taking her in his arms Daniel suggests they have a rest before getting ready for tonight's party. Suddenly feeling shy Milly argues that she has too much to do but Daniel silences her with a tender kiss.

"I want to lie down with my wife in my arms for an hour. Maybe we'll doze, but certainly we'll relax and get some rest. We can get comfortable on the couch in the sitting-room."

"Oh! Oh yes, that would work... I thought–" she breaks off sharply and Daniel enjoys the sight of her scarlet cheeks.

"When we celebrate our wedding night I won't be rushing, sweetheart. You have nothing to fear and nothing to worry about, okay?" He tips her chin up and savors her expression, a mixture of apprehension and anticipation.

When Stephen brings Samuel home after their lunch his booming voice has everyone stirring. They find Daniel stretched out on the couch with Milly curled between him and the sofa back.

"Wake up, sleepyheads," he calls. "You've got some news to share with the rest of the family."

Samuel is equally enthusiastic to share the news and he calls up the stairs: *hey everybody get down here, we've got good news to celebrate!*

Esther arrives first asking *what? why? what's going on?* Samuel gives her a hug and swings her around. His joy is infectious and she jumps up and down in excitement. Amos and Nora follow closely also eager to know *what's up?*

Now that his audience is gathered a beaming Samuel takes hold of Milly and Daniel's hands and lifting them up in triumph shouts *say hello to Mr and Mrs Daniel Young!*

The moment of stunned silence breaks with Esther shrieking *omigod you're married for real?* Nora's warm *oh how wonderful,* and Amos clapping Daniel on the back with a hearty *bro, sweet!*

Hugs, kisses, and handshakes are exchanged and even Esther's wail of *but I wanted to be your bridesmaid* is half-hearted.

"That's why you both got dressed up today! Tell us everything!" Nora insists, dragging Milly to sit beside her on the sofa.

"Yeah, why the secrecy and rush?" asks Amos.

"There's so much going on right now with the holidays that throwing a wedding reception into the mix is just too much so that's why we kept it secret," explains Milly.

"And I didn't want to wait any longer to make Milly my wife," Daniel states simply. "No year-long engagement followed by a fall wedding so that explains the rush."

"You realize tongues will wag–" begins Nora.

Laughing Daniel confides "Oh we're counting on it!"

"Yes, I expect all the gossips will come by the Farm Shop in five or six months to look me over," Milly agrees, giggling.

"Ha! you're so right!" Nora exclaims.

Milly nods adding: "And I plan to maneuver every one of them into making a purchase while they're there."

Getting into the spirit of the joke Esther says: "You can hide behind the counter and they'll eventually have to buy something or leave."

"Oh that's a great idea, Esther. What a way to get our little café off the ground! I'll stay half-hidden until they order something and then I'll say *take a seat and I'll bring it to you.* That's perfect!"

With a loud sigh Stephen says: "I should be discouraging you from teasing your neighbors but..." he pauses to grin and add: "I'll be dropping by myself to enjoy the show!"

Hannah and Jim arrive to the sound of laughter and are soon happily congratulating the newlyweds. "How exciting! Tonight we'll have more to celebrate than just the new year," says Hannah, "Are we keeping it secret until you make an announcement?"

"Yes, good idea," says Samuel. Esther is already busy texting the news to Amelia so her father interrupts her saying: "Tell Amelia to keep it quiet until we can do the big reveal." That appeals to the teenager who now swears her friend to secrecy.

Everyone is in good spirits as they prepare for the party. Milly is too busy in the kitchen to feel nervous. It helps that Daniel constantly finds excuses to keep in contact by touching her hand or smoothing back her hair or planting quick kisses on her forehead, cheek, and nose. She feels very connected to him.

Milly has just changed into her party dress when Nora taps on the door. Invited in she brandishes a bag of cosmetics saying: "I paid attention to that make-up stylist we had for my wedding and I'm going to copy what she did, okay?"

Touched by the kindness Milly gets emotional saying: "Aww, that's so sweet of you, Nora! And yes please, because all I can manage is mascara and you always look fantastic."

Hearing their chatter Esther knocks on the open door and seeing the make-up session demands to join in. "You're both my sister-in-laws, or is it sisters-in-law? so we're all family."

"That's right, and we have to maintain our reputation as *those lovely Young women*," Nora states.

It's a cheerful sight that greets the three men when they converge in the hallway. They're met with radiant smiles as they compliment the beauty of their girls.

Samuel is barely audible when he breathes "Family... sons and daughters," his eyes bright with emotion.

"Hey!" says Amos, "Now I understand what you meant about not waiting to update your driver's license. You two are so sneaky!"

Less than an hour later guests start arriving. True to her word Miz Tally attends the party and is one of the first through the door, accompanied by Janice Peart. The elderly lady is in high spirits but her stay at the nursing home shows in weight loss and a look of fragility.

Everyone flocks round her to check in and wish her the best for the new year. Her teacup and cake-plate are kept filled while her ear hears all the local news supplemented by supposition and surmise.

Spotting an opportunity to catch her attention Milly and Daniel sit down on the couch beside her upright chair.

"My dears! I heard the wonderful news of your engagement and—"

"Wedding," interrupts Daniel.

"Well yes, a wedding, when are you getting married?"

"Today. This morning, actually," replies Milly.

"Sweetheart I think it was afternoon by time I said *I do*," Daniel corrects her.

"What on earth are you two saying... did you get... are you married already?"

"We did, we are!" the two chorus, beaming. "Congratulate us!"

The old lady's eyes well up with tears as she gives her heartfelt blessing. "Oh my dears, I wish you both a long and happy married life. I just knew you would bring good luck to The Cove and to the Young's Milly Clarke. Oops, it's Milly Young now! However I'd also like to box your ears Daniel because I so wanted to attend your wedding."

Daniel is unrepentant as he says in a sing-song voice: "Sorry-not-sorry! " and a laugh explodes out of Milly. She quickly covers her mouth but can't hide the gleeful sparkle in her eyes.

I've never seen Daniel like this before! she exclaims to herself. *He's usually so sober and serious and self-contained but this... wow. It's wonderful to see this side of him. Can it really be just because we got married?*

She has to focus her mind to return to the conversation and hears him say: "...every minute we spent not married had me worried she'd change her mind, Miz Tally. Underneath this demure exterior lies a fierce and spirited nature."

Looking into the surprised face of his bride Daniel tells her: "I've got you now and I'm never letting go."

Miz Tally sighs happily hearing his words. She remembers Milly's disappointment two weeks ago at Daniel's apparent inability to express his affection.

Milly is breathless with overwhelming emotion threatening her with a silly urge to cry. She's brought back to earth when a querulous voice demands: "What's this I hear? You're married? We've only just heard about the engagement!"

Janice Peart's anger is ridiculous and Milly has to bite her lip to keep the laughter inside. With his gaze focused on her mouth Daniel is prompted to swoop down for a kiss.

A chuckling Miz Tally exclaims: "There's your answer, Janice!"

Before Janice can spread the news Samuel calls for everyone's attention. Announcing that he spent his lunch-hour witnessing a wedding ceremony with a flourish he brings forward *the newest Mr. and Mrs. Young of Sweet Berry Cove.*

The decibel level of the party skyrockets with applause accompanied by shouted *congratulations!* and the New Year's Eve celebration becomes even more festive. Miz Tally leaves before midnight, tired but pleased, and everyone is thankful to have seen her enjoying herself.

Before her friend left Milly witnessed a touching encounter between Miz Tally and Helena Larch. She saw the old woman take hold of Helena's hand saying:

"My dear I'm delighted to see you so happy and filled with love."

Knowing she's never been much in favor with the older women of The Cove a slightly disconcerted Helena turns to her husband explaining: "Oh well, that's all Chris's doing—"

Interrupting, Miz Tally says: "Naturally Christopher loves you but I'm talking about the love inside you, my dear.

Helena, I have done you a disservice imagining that you were chasing a mirage and your marriage wouldn't last. I'm so glad to be proved wrong. You're dealing with an incredible challenge and the strength you're showing is admirable.

The compassionate love you've extended to young Amelia is heartwarming. It won't be easy but it's obvious to me that the three of you will make a go of it and I wish you every happiness."

Helena is speechless but her eyes shine with joy. She quickly bends and bestows a quick kiss on Miz Tally's cheek. Chris gently places his hand on top of the elderly lady's and wishes her *good health and a very happy new year.*

After the midnight countdown when cheers have welcomed in 2024 Daniel pulls Milly close for a kiss. He gently brushes his lips against hers murmuring *Happy New Year, wife* and Milly melts into him. *Oh husband*, she sighs feeling his arms tighten around her.

Honeymoon in Morro Bay

Milly and Daniel's embrace is interrupted by Samuel who takes hold of their arms to lead them through the kitchen out to the yard. Stephen is there holding warm coats and a suitcase.

"Don't worry Milly, it was Nora who packed it, not me!" he chuckles.

Looking from one man to the other Daniel asks: "What's all this about, Dad?"

"It's our wedding present to you. We've booked you youngsters a quick getaway at Morro Bay. The hotels were solidly booked for the holidays but we've found you a guest house on Airbnb. The place looks great on the website, it's small but cute and cozy. They've even got Christmas lights up!"

"Where - or what - is Morro Bay?" asks Milly.

"It's a year-round tourist spot with loads of art galleries and artisan's shops, rentals of everything from bikes to kayaks to kites. You'll love it. This past week they've had daytime temperatures of 60 to 65," answers Stephen with enthusiasm. "Here Daniel, give me your phone and I'll put the address into your GPS. It's only a fifteen-minute drive, tops."

"Wow this is... I don't know what to say Dad... Stephen..." Daniel is at a loss for words, this gift is so unexpected but very welcome.

"Just enjoy yourselves! This is an important time for the two of you so make some great memories."

"Oh! that's so nice of you!" says Milly, her face alight with excitement.

"We'll take your new car if that's okay with you, hon?"

"Of course it's okay but would you mind doing the driving there? I'm not as confident driving in the dark to somewhere I've never been before."

Daniel takes a moment to unpack that sentence before assuring her: "Sweetheart, I'm happy to drive you anywhere, anytime."

With Samuel's blessing they don't go back into the house to say goodnight to their guests, choosing to discreetly slip away. They're on the road in no time.

They encounter almost no traffic during the drive and Daniel compliments how well the new car handles the curvy road.

"I thought I'd feel cramped sitting here but it's much roomier than it looks like from the outside."

"I know, Cindy is perfect."

Her husband chuckles at the idea of Milly naming her car.

"You know, I really was remiss in not planning tonight better. I can't believe I didn't realize what... where we... oh! oh no Milly, I am sorry."

She turns to him with a quizzical look.

"I forgot about how you were so excited listening to Nora talk about their exotic honeymoon trip and I've offered you nothing. I was just in such a rush to marry you that I wasn't thinking straight about anything else."

Smiling sweetly Milly simply states: "Well then, it's a good thing Samuel and Stephen arranged this getaway for us."

"It really, really is," Daniel says with a rueful laugh. "We can still plan something, whether it's relaxing on a tropical island or traveling across the world to go sightseeing in a capital city... what would you prefer? Hey! have you ever been on a plane?"

"No, so why not plan on both? But for some future date, not yet. Right now I just want to spend a long weekend enjoying my husband's company and having him all to myself. Then we'll head back home to get the Farm Shop Café off the ground."

"Both? Ha! I like your way of thinking, wife! Especially since you've got all that money to spend."

"I do and oh! should I have arranged a honeymoon trip for us, Daniel?"

"No sweetheart, that really is the groom's job and I'm only teasing about your money. That's yours to spend on yourself, I've got plenty to keep the both of us comfortable."

"Oh Daniel my money is ours, really and truly, when you said that about it coming between us—"

He interrupts to apologize for ever throwing her inheritance in her face. "I was thoughtless and insensitive, Milly. I'm really sorry for what I said. I think you getting what was always yours by right is a wonderful thing."

She looks down in her lap and notices her hands twisting together. Forcing herself to still she quietly says: "It *is* wonderful, it's a gift from my parents. Although I never knew them finding out that they cared about me, loved me, enough to prepare for my future well... honestly Daniel, words can't express how good that makes me feel."

"Milly you really are the best and I'm a very lucky man."

She swats him playfully but he hears a telltale sniff and knows she is feeling as emotional as he is. It's been a day - a few days, actually - of new and overwhelming thoughts, feelings, sensations... it's been a lot. They need this quiet time to be together just the two of them.

"Oh I just thought... where are we going to sleep when we're back at the farmhouse? I mean, we don't still keep our own bedrooms... or do we?"

"You move into my room with me. It's bigger and the bed is way bigger than yours. It will only be until our own home is built and that will happen quickly, believe me."

The GPS on Daniel's phone now announces *your destination is on the right*.

Their rental is on the outskirts of the Bay but still within walking distance of the beach. Looking out over the water they see it's full of boats all sporting colorful lights and they hear echoes of music from a variety of sources.

They pause at the cottage door to absorb the lively party atmosphere and catch the grand finale of a New Year's fireworks display. In the ensuing quiet they hear a light tinkling from a delicate set of wind-chimes, adding to the night's marvels.

"Daniel this night has been just as good as any wedding reception could be," declares Milly.

Nodding in agreement Daniel punches the code into the keypad and the door unlocks. Scooping Milly up into his arms he carries her over the threshold. Her happy squeals blend tunefully with his triumphant laughter.

"Oh Daniel, this really does feel like a fairy tale."

"That's exactly what this is Milly, because you're my happily ever after."

"Forever and ever, amen!"

From the Author

Dear Reader:

Thank you so much for choosing *"Finding Forever in Sweet Berry Cove"*. I thoroughly enjoyed writing more about Milly and Daniel's story, and hope this book met your expectations.

Please consider leaving a rating or a review. These provide helpful information to other readers, and assist authors in rankings.

In grateful appreciation,

Ness Woodberry

Also by Ness Woodberry

Sweet Berry Cove

Finding Forever in Sweet Berry Cove

Standalone

Finding Love in Sweet Berry Cove